THE CHRONICLES OF LEVI & JONES

The Chronicles of Levi & Jones

RYAN CRAWFORD

Published by Crawford Adventures 2023
Arcadia, FL

Library of Congress Control Number: 2023902678

Cover Design by Rebecca McGillicuddy of NoirArtist Illustrations

Paperback ISBN: 979-8-9875549-1-3

eBook ISBN: 979-8-9875549-2-0

Printed in the United States of America by IngramSpark

I dedicate this book to my wife Anna and my mother, Shellsie.

Chapter 1

Warm air blows along the eastern coast early in the morning. The calm waves of the ocean move in unison as the whitecaps break against the rocky shoreline. As the day begins, the sunrise casts crisp shadows on buildings, trees, and bustling traffic. Birds and waterfowl fly in slow motion across the skyline. Early risers are already out and about, walking their dogs along the park paths as they do every morning. Life's regular, mundane routine remains slow and relaxed as everyone carries on with their lives. It's business as usual at Binsley High School, the town's oldest public institution, which sits right on the seashore with ocean views from most rooms. Students chat with their friends in the busy hallways as they walk to class. In this small town, something extraordinary, magical, and life-altering is about to happen, with no one suspecting. Students are rifling through books and papers in many rooms while carrying on with conversations or looking at their cellphones. Most pupils don't even pay attention to their instructors or lesson plans. The early school bell signals a shortened day, beginning a three-day break. Mrs. Barren, one of the few English teachers, closes her textbook on her desk.

"Okay, everyone, I dismiss class. Enjoy your time off and study for next week's test."

Students, thrilled, gather books and bags, cheering. In the hallways, many varieties of current music are playing from various Bluetooth speakers and headphones. The area fills with kids grabbing their stuff and closing their lockers. Unwavering enthusiasm is in the air, as most are eager about leaving early that Thursday morning. Many students walk towards the buses. Staff members and chaperons watch the horizon beyond the transportation as the kids scramble around the schoolyard to find their bus or ride home. They are not paying attention to the students or the gentle waves of the sea. Instead, they focus on what is forming in their field of vision. Something mammoth is brewing as the bright sun loses its brilliance under the growing cloud cover. Most bus routes are local, but two vehicles must travel to the remote rural parts of nearby towns.

After some time, school bus number 37, which travels the furthest from school, drops off its remaining passengers. Levi Lumboss makes his way off the bus, which stops in front of his house on the corner of Keelstrom Street. The entrance to his home faces the embankment, while the right side offers a view of weathered wooden docks where majestic schooners and rugged fishing boats are moored. He carries his backpack to his front door while waving to his friend.

"I'll call you later."

He halts a few feet from his entrance, looking up at the sky. Unlike the typical hustle and bustle of sailors, dock workers, and shipwrights, he finds the harbor town unusually still. He watches a colony of seagulls and pelicans fly overhead. Small waves and rippling water sounds that once filled the air now fall silent. It's like nature pressed the mute button to quiet its normal background noise. He looks around the neighboring homes and notices no one outside or any activity. Levi watches black clouds forming in the distance, and even though something feels amiss, he blows them off and returns to his happy thoughts of his early dismissal. While fetching his key, he checks the mailbox, grabs the contents, and enters his residence. Scanning through the letters, he places his backpack atop the kitchen counter.

"Nothing for me."

He heads to the refrigerator for a snack. Levi stays in the house alone for a short time as his parents work to support the family. He plops himself on the sofa to watch some TV. Grabbing the remote control, he can't push any buttons because a loud crack of thunder startles him. Jumping off the couch, he runs upstairs and stands in front of some windows. The sky is alive with manifesting clouds, expanding and morphing before his eyes.

Wind and heavy rain begin within minutes. This sudden change in weather patterns skyrockets the size and violence of the crashing surges in the harbor. Utility wires whip back and forth against the waterlogged utility poles as intermittent sparks shoot out of the dated electric transformers that energize homes and businesses. The old fishing boats and schooners of Coralbrink sway against the docks, their thick ropes strained to the limit as they endure the relentless waves.

Levi looks at the clock, wondering when his parents will return home from work. Leo, his dad, is a small charter plane copilot for a company that delivers fresh fish and seafood daily to higher-end restaurants. Despite delivering cargo hundreds of miles away, he typically returns before sunset. His mom, Lauren, works part-time as a successful travel agent in the neighboring town of Netinburg. Levi notices the clouds, rain, and darkness spreading across the area at a rapid pace as he snatches his mobile phone. Winds slap the side of the house as the shutters open and close.

He tries sending a text to his parents, only to receive an error as the cell signal is intermittent. Levi's mother is looking out the front window of the travel agency's office, noticing that the weather is becoming dreadful. She unsuccessfully tries to call and text Levi, as her cell signal is also weak and intermittent. There is an increasing amount of wind in Netinburg, which blows down a large oak tree, blocking the entrance to the office. Authorities are shutting down the roads as the storm is growing. Police cars drive down the streets, avoiding vast piles of debris as they announce on their loud horns that everyone must stay indoors. Lauren talks to her co-workers while trying to remain calm.

"I can't get a hold of my son, and I've got to go home. I hope he is okay."

Her peers try to console her as she sobs. The landline and cellphone outages cause office operations to stop. Meanwhile, Levi turns on the TV and tries flipping through several channels. The screen displays more interference than weather forecasts. During all the fast-growing commotion, there is a sudden frantic banging on the front door. Levi runs down the stairs and looks through the peephole. His neighbor and best friend, Jones Jackson, is clinging to a broken umbrella while jumping up and down. In a surprising turn of events, Jones, a geeky African American teenager, stands toe to toe with Levi, a geeky Caucasian teenager of smaller stature. They're both thirteen and share a birthday. They have been inseparable best friends ever since!

"Open the door, Levi! I'm getting soaked!"

Levi opens the door while leaning against it so the wind won't blow it open. Jones stumbles into the house, fighting to close his collapsed umbrella.

"Good grief, where did this nasty weather come from?"

"A tremendous storm is coming, and I can't reach anyone. My cell doesn't have a signal, and the TV isn't working."

While shaking the water from his outdated cell phone, Jones complains.

"My phone isn't working either."

Levi closes the door.

"I can't call my parents to find out where they are."

Jones is the only child of a widowed parent.

"My mom isn't home, and I can't call her either."

Jones's father, Charlie, was a police officer who passed away in the line of duty. Jones's mother, Samantha, is also trying to reach him, but has no luck. She is also a police officer in the town of Coralbrink. Her boss has ordered her to close the roads and maintain control with the help of her co-workers, but she becomes frustrated. As Samantha's police car sits in the middle of a street with its lights flashing, she is on her cell phone trying to reach Jones. Her partner ensures residents move to a safer location. In frustration, she shakes the phone and throws it in the passenger seat while her concern grows.

"Darn it. I've taught Jones what to do in emergencies, and I know he will be all right. He's an intelligent kid. I need to stay calm and keep my wits about me."

With a worried look, she returns her attention to her work. Damaging winds and flaring fires overwhelm her as everything shuts down. Meanwhile, Levi stares out the front window.

"It's getting worse out there. I bet this will become a hurricane or something."

"I'm nervous, Levi. What do we do?"

Before Levi can answer, the loud siren of the severe weather system startles him as it activates around town. Its haunting tone shakes the boys to the core. The rain grows heavier and the sky darker as they run from window to window in the house. A few once upright trees are swaying sideways in the wind. Waves from the angry ocean pummel the docks and shoreline. Thunder rumbles and explodes in the sky as lightning strikes a few feet from Levi's house, igniting a small part of the dock. In a panic, Levi screams.

"We need to take cover!"

Jones looks around the house for somewhere to escape.

"Where do we go? Do we get in the closet or something?"

Debris fills the air while the storm causes great destruction. Boats are flipping over and capsizing. Parts of cars, bikes, and other equipment shoot through the air as if launched from a cannon. Streetlights and lamp posts detach from their bases and collide with buildings. A few houses rip from their foundations and toss around in the air. The sound of the weather's power drowns out the sounds of carnage. With a thunderous boom and crash, one window in the front of Levi's house shatters inward as the gale force blows a boat paddle through the air. Picture frames and collectibles fall off the wall as the wind whips through the house, while other windows vibrate as the air pressure changes. Levi sees in his peripheral vision several chunks of wood, metal, and wreckage flying around outside. The boys, frightened and confused, scream while running through the house. Levi grabs Jones's hand and runs for the basement door.

"Oh my gosh, it's a hurricane! This way! Follow me!"

Levi's dad made a rule preventing him from venturing into the basement. However, in this case, he disobeys and pulls hard on the door. Bursting through the entrance, the boys fill with more adrenaline. They pull the door shut and make their way down the stairs. It is a dark, compact space filled with old moving boxes, some furniture, and an enormous tool chest.

The only light is a flickering bulb hanging from the ceiling. The boys listen to the destruction happening above them. Jones feels troubled and apprehensive.

"Where do we take cover?"

"I don't know. My father always told me never to come down here."

Little do the boys know that the upcoming hurricane will be the most intense flash storm ever recorded, and its relentless wrath is heading straight for their town. Driven by the loud crashes from upstairs, the boy's panic as glass shatters and furniture slams to the floor. With a gentle quake, the earth trembles, adding to the chaos. A wild gust of wind, heavy rain, and swirling debris breach the basement as the door bursts open. Levi yells as they scramble behind the large tool chest for cover.

"Over here!"

They hear sparks and explosions as the hurricane churns away at the defenseless town. The boys hunker down behind the tool chest.

"I'm scared, Jones! Oh, my gosh!"

They sit in the fetal position with their hands over their heads as they huddle together. The ceiling over the basement breaks apart as the dim gray daylight from above pokes through the timbers that make up the weakening floor. Boards fly in the air with the force of a rocket. In a dramatic display, a massive timber log from the local sawmill crashes through the basement ceiling in a stunning explosion, narrowly missing the boys. It penetrates the concrete and plaster wall, revealing decaying wooden boards beneath. In one large gust, the floor above rips away from the foundation. Jones peers through the gap between the boards, spotting a mysterious underground space hidden behind the aged planks. He forces the boards apart, creating enough space to crawl through, then signals Levi to follow.

"Come on!"

Another log slams into the tool chest, forcing it back and almost crushing the boys as they crawl behind the boards. The tool chest temporarily shields the new entrance as tons of water and debris cover it. They don't know the storm destroyed the rest of the house.

Chapter 2

Soaked and frightened, the boys struggle to comprehend and endure the situation. Levi assesses the state of his best friend.

"Jeez, that was close. Are you OK?"

"Ya, I guess so."

Behind the boards lay a dark, narrow void, a rocky passage carved from stone and earth. The rock formations emit a soft orange phosphorescent glow in the five-by-five square tunnel. Mesmerized, Levi and Jones scrambled to their knees. Filled with fear and awe, Jones questions their predicament.

"What is this place?"

Fearful, they ignore the sounds of destruction emanating from the other side of the vibrating tool chest. The storm's force remains clear as water seeps beneath the tool chest and into the tunnel. Levi tries to push back into the basement, but nothing moves.

"I can't move it! It's too heavy."

Jones assisted his friend.

"Here, let me try."

After Jones's unsuccessful attempt, Levi takes out his cracked-screen cell phone and turns on the flashlight, redirecting their attention to the passage ahead. In the darkness, they notice dense spiderwebs, dirt, scars on rocks caused by pickaxes, and the shadows of ancient rock formations. Levi feels both fear and awe.

"I've never seen anything like this before. Where are we?"

"I don't know. It's some old tunnel. Are you sure you're OK, buddy?"

Levi nods and replies.

"I think so, but I don't know what to do."

A dominant foreground noise, startling Jones, reaches the boys' ears.

"What's that sound?"

Levi gazes ahead, shushing Jones as he attempts to discern the source and nature of the sound. They can't see over six feet in front of them.

"It sounds like... It sounds like running water and lots of it. Maybe like a river or stream."

Jones becomes more frustrated.

"River? Stream? How are those going to be underground?"

"I don't know. But we need to get out of here."

The boys crawl forward on their hands and knees. Grossed out by spiderwebs, scurrying rats, and other menacing-looking pests that inhabit the tunnel, they inch further down. The rushing water's sound grows more intense, and the number of spiderwebs and rats multiplies as the boys move forward. Levi complains as they struggle to evade the pests because of the inadequate lighting in the passage.

"We have to find a way out. Argh, I hate rats!"

They continue to crawl, following the sound of water. Little do the boys realize they are descending deeper underground. Jones feels a tightening in his chest, and a knot of anxiety is forming.

"This is scary."

With the dim light from Levi's phone, the guys attempt to discern what lies in the distance, aided only by the glowing rocks in the tunnel. Levi tries to apply his scientific reasoning to the situation.

"This must be a secret passageway."

Almost immediately, the sound of the water ceases, and an eerie silence envelops the tunnel. Jones is confused.

"W... what happened to the water?"

A deep, eerie, horrifying moan coming from a distance interrupts him mid-question. The boys freeze in their tracks, their fear escalating as the moan grows louder. Jones enters a state of panic.

"Let's go back the other way."

"We can't! The exit is blocked. We have got to keep moving."

"Are you crazy, Levi? I'm not going down there. Didn't you hear that moan?"

"Well, we can't stay here."

As they continue to listen to the low-tone moan, they notice a small, translucent light-green orb floating from the right side of the tunnel to the left. At that moment, Levi panics.

"Did you see that? Come on! We have to keep going. We will die if we stay here."

The orb vanishes as quickly as it appeared, and the sound of water in the distance returns. Meanwhile, the storm intensifies, causing the house's basement to fill with storm water. Nearby homes and businesses are being obliterated by the hurricane, leaving a path of destruction. An intense explosion, followed by a crack, echoes through the tunnel, and the sound of massive amounts of water flowing into the tunnel behind the tool chest begins. The boys watch in horror as the small trickle of water transforms into a raging underground tsunami, engulfing the tunnel. Crawling faster into the dark tunnel, Jones yells at Levi.

"Go! Go! Go!"

The water catches up with them, flipping them onto their backs and sweeping the two down the tunnel like a terrifying water slide into the abyss. As the water carries them down the spooky shaft, Levi can't hold on to his phone as he screams. As they pick up speed, the water flings their bodies from side to side. The water gains pressure and speed from the tunnel that extends deeper into the earth.

During the journey into darkness, their arms and legs flail back and forth. Levi and Jones yell bloody murder at the top of their lungs as they struggle to keep their heads above water. The water roars, and the eerie moans of something alarming grow louder. The tunnel swerves left and right as the boys' speed increases with the rising water pressure. A blurry, translucent green head materializes out of nowhere and races past the boys as their water ride continues. A loud, eerie, and deep moan resonates from the head as it glides past the boys once more before vanishing into the tunnel wall. The flow slows as the tunnel slopes uphill. Once again, the head appears out of nowhere, keeping pace with the boys. Its foul, crooked mouth drips with slimy saliva, exposing its dirty, broken teeth. It threatens them.

"Go away!"

Panic fills them as the ride approaches its end. The head grumbles as its sinister eyes roll back in the grotesque, deformed face.

"Go back!"

As the ghostly head nears the sliding boys, it enlarges. Before vanishing back into the tunnel wall, it continues to menace them.

"This is your last warning!"

Soon, the boys enter a glowing chamber at the end of the shaft. After the moans stop, only the sound of water is audible. The ground on which they are sliding disappears with a swooshing wave, and the boys launch over a twenty-foot-high waterfall that cascades into a large, murky lagoon. They both yell in terror as they plunge into the deep water. Both of their heads emerge. Jones screams, struggling to stay afloat.

"Help! Levi! Help!"

He isn't a strong swimmer, but neither is Levi. With a flurry of splashing and kicking, they grasp each other and make their way to the shore of this open cave. They pull themselves up onto the flat rocky area, coughing and gasping as they regain their breath. Levi spits water from his mouth.

"Oh my gosh, this is insane."

Jones agrees.

"I want to go home! This is a nightmare."

Levi coughs while surveying the peculiar cave, which emanates an ominous orange glow. The powerful flowing waterfall envelops the silence in this ancient subterranean cave adorned with thousand-year-old stalactites and stalagmites. Jones is in awe.

"Wow, look at this place. Is there any way out of here?"

The cavernous room is immense, large enough to return any echo twice, with even eerier delivery the second time. The rock formations rise thirty feet, and the guys cannot discern the width or diameter of the area because of the darkness at the outer edges. Though the waterfall continues to flow, it loses some pressure and slows down. The warm orange glow emanating from the rock formations prevents the area from being too dark. Levi and Jones pull themselves to their feet and gaze into the ancient void. Levi is dizzy from the experience.

"Where the heck are we?"

Jones answers his friend, not realizing the sea had swept away his house.

"Let's find a way out of here. I want to go home."

They do not know what to do or where to go. Levi cries, glancing around desperately for a solution.

"We are trapped! There is no way out of here."

Panic overtakes the boys' emotions, and both cry. Amidst their dread, something mysterious occurs. The waterfall slows even further and then stops flowing. From the silence, the eerie moan they had heard returns. The murky pool of water they emerged from glows green, with a translucent orb drifting just beneath the surface.

Levi and Jones freeze in fear, their eyes and mouths wide open, yet unable to say anything. They have witnessed nothing paranormal in their lives. Fear spreads across the boys' faces as the orb breaks the surface of the water. It emits a chilling humming sound as it approaches them. The eerie sphere hovers above the two, making crackling noises reminiscent of a hot sparkler as it shifts color from green to white. The light from the orb is so bright that the boys have to cover their eyes. A gruff, mean-looking man with a thick mustache and greasy streaks of dirt covering his face wears a heavy scowl as his torso moves. He glares down at poor Levi and Jones.

Chapter 3

Levi and Jones tremble in place, their jaws nearly touching the ground as their eyes widen wide. The glowing apparition maintains eye contact as it opens its grotesque mouth and speaks in a slow, deep, resonant voice.

"Who are you?"

"I am J... Jones... Jackson, and t... this is Levi."

"How did you get down here?"

"There is a storm, and we were hiding in my basement. The storm broke the wall, revealing a tunnel we climbed into."

A heavy scowl replaces the expression of surprise as the miner's brow furrows.

"Silence! Why are you here? This is not where you belong. This is your final resting place."

The thought of being stuck here made Levi cry.

"No, please! We didn't mean to be here."

Jones also pleaded with the specter.

"We want to go home! Please don't hurt us."

A haunting neon green glow emanates from the ghost's eyes as he rises higher above the boys.

"You have disturbed my grave, and now you will join me."

Both boys sank to their knees as Levi kept pleading for their case.

"Please, no! We want to leave, but we don't have a clue how to leave."

"He's right. We want to leave. Please help us. Tell us how to get out of here."

The ghost falls silent and glares at the boys as it hovers above them. The scowl on his face grows angrier than before. Shooting stars emanating from the spirit's body increase as he rests his hand on his ghostly chin, appearing to contemplate the situation.

"You are the ones who have disturbed me! I should curse your souls for eternity, but then again, how could two wimpy kids find their way down here? You look too young to know about the legend. I may spare you from my fate only if you do something for me."

Levi's eyes perk wide open.

"What is it? Please tell us."

Jones takes part in the groveling.

"Whatever you want, we will do it. We just want to go home."

The ghost lethargically lowers himself to the boys' level. His worn boots hit the ground. He stands seven feet tall. The spirit glares at the boys as he places his hands on his waist and squints one eye. Their gaze fixed on the prospector, the boys remained kneeling. The miner's bright glow softens as he looks down at the boys and shares the legend in his slow, whispered tone. A dull white cloud appears on the side of the ghost.

"It has been more than a century since I was alive on this forsaken earth. I accepted a job at the Crenshaw Mining Company."

Images appear in the cloud, and the boys can see the prospector as he did over a century ago. The pictures keep changing as the apparition shares his story.

"They hired me as the foreman of an elite group of men whose talents included deep excavation and exploration into the earth. The owner of the mining company was Orville Crenshaw, a renowned archaeologist who was a mysterious man. Rumors circulated he was studying ancient black magic. Orville searched for many years for hidden wealth and one day stumbled upon a map written on ancient parchment on his adventures and journeys around the world. The map supposedly leads to a powerful, inexplicable treasure. An object that contains unimaginable abilities discovered by ancient peoples many millennia ago."

He pauses for a moment to wipe the thick saliva from his rotting lips.

"It was my job to find this bounty of riches. Crenshaw gave me this small green stone amulet attached to this chain to wear around my neck as a promise of tremendous fortune and prosperity. Being a superstitious man, he told me to never take it off or terrible luck would befall my men and me. Leading with a heavy fist, he had me oversee my group charged with digging a mine shaft to the treasure that's rumored to be buried deep in the earth by these ancient peoples."

He turns away in disgust before resuming his story.

"I did not want to continue because my men were exhausted, hurt, and dying as they dug deeper. I became frustrated and asked myself why we would work so hard to dig deep into the earth and not know what we were looking for. Crenshaw was cruel, mean, and secretive about everything. He promised my team and me untold wealth upon successfully finding whatever we were looking for. He said we would discover what we were seeking when we found it."

The spirit directed his scowl at the two teens.

"The old legend says that this treasure possesses no wealth but is magical."

The boys focus intently on the images in the cloud but cannot discern the blurry image of the treasure.

"One day, while my men were removing rock and earth by filling mine carts pulled by a mule, a strange green mist filled the mine shafts. It's mysterious because the mist did not come from anywhere, but then, in the next second, it just existed everywhere.. Most of my men started passing out and died, and the others, lucky enough to make it out, soon died from exposure to this mysterious vapor. Rushing into the entrance, I covered my face with my handkerchief to save more men, but soon I became overwhelmed and passed out. I fell down a deep shaft, never to be seen again. When I became spiritually conscious of my death, I discovered I had gained new abilities. You may call them magical powers, but I view them as an extension of my body."

The spirit pauses as a look of disgust covers its face.

"It must have been the green amulet that cursed me to stay here in the afterlife, as I am weak when distant from the mine. Blast that Crenshaw! He must have expected what would happen. Crenshaw, who was selfish, didn't want to suffer public humiliation and ridicule, so he soon hired more men to hide everything by blowing up the entrance. He proclaimed that if he couldn't have the power, no one would. The town of Coralbrink was eventually constructed atop the mine and the burial sites of many of my men. I've been doomed to haunt this place for eternity. You stumbled into one of the few air shafts we dug. This is why you are here."

Levi pleads with the ghost.

"What do you want us to do?"

"I cannot rest, and I am cursed to remain here until my job is over. You will need to continue where I left off. I don't know what the treasure looks like, but you have to find it, or you will join me in this earthly crypt till the end of time."

Levi gazes at Jones with a pout.

"We have no choice. We either do it or we will die."

"Are you kidding me? We will die anyway! Oh my gosh, no! I don't want to die."

Levi comforts Jones and assures the ghost that they will try. Jones then pleads with the ghost.

"But how do we escape?"

"You have accepted the task; if you fail, death will be your escape."

The ghost wails as he lifts his left arm and points to a section of the solid rock wall.

"Your journey begins here. Good luck."

Jones looks at Levi with a confused expression.

"What are we looking at? It's just a rock wall."

Levi questions the spooky miner.

"I don't understand. How does this start with a rock wall?"

The miner let out a deep, horrific-sounding laugh and faded into the darkness of the water. Suddenly, a tremendous underground earthquake shakes the chamber where the boys are. Rock and debris tumble from the cave's summit like a terrifying storm that flips the chamber upside down. Chunks of falling boulders obliterate the waterfall entrance and fill the dark lagoon. Levi and Jones scramble for cover behind a fallen boulder. Levi yells in terror.

"Ah, what's happening now?"

A bright dot appears on the wall near the cave's ceiling. Starting from that point, it moves in a zigzag pattern to the bottom of the wall. A deep crack appears in the rock over the pattern created by the bright dot. In the region where the crack formed, massive slabs of rock forcefully slide apart. The glow of the stones in the cavernous chamber fades, leaving the area dark. After the ground stops shaking and the debris settles, a dull light emerges from behind those slabs, revealing another chamber.

Chapter 4

Levi and Jones stand up, regain their composure, and dust themselves off. Jones assesses the condition of his friend as he gazes at the new opening that leads deeper into their adventure.

"Are you okay?"

Levi brushes the dirt and rocks from his hair.

"I think so. This is crazy."

Gathering their courage, the boys stand side by side, examining the new entrance with a soft light shining through it. Levi shares his thoughts.

"Well, we'd better go if we are getting out of here."

"Aren't you worried we will not survive this?"

"We can't go the other way, so let's be brave and do this."

As they approach the entrance, they navigate through the rubble.

They both look at each other and gulp as Levi displays his bravery.

"Here goes nothing."

Walking past the slabs, they find themselves in another chamber. However, this chamber is longer and narrower than the previous area, with a lower ceiling. The chamber contains old mining tools and broken equipment. Gradually, the guys walk past and over the objects in front of them. They discover more scattered pitchforks, shovels, mine cart parts. The historical discovery amazes Levi.

"Wow, look at all this stuff!"

They stop moving as fear sets in. Jones spots something in the distance.

"What's that over there?"

He points to a skeleton lying on its back, still clad in tattered miners' clothing and an old cap that covers the skull. Levi tries to avoid staring at it.

"That must be one of the miners' men that died here."

The boys trudge about five feet past the skeleton when they stop dead in their tracks. They overhear an eerie popping noise behind them. Slowly, they turn around to behold the skeleton they just passed, standing upright and pointing beyond them. Moments later, as the skeleton disintegrates into a heap of bones and fabric, they let out a scream. They turn around and run to the opposite side of the chamber, stumbling over historical artifacts.

"Oh, my gosh! Oh, my gosh. Jones! What the heck is that?"

Jones is so terrified that he can only mumble words. After a few minutes of shaking and heavy breathing, they calm down and continue on. A rusted, partially obscured mine track lies at the end of the chamber. An old wooden mine cart rests on its side, decaying and dry, held together only by rusty bolts and metal trim. Levi and Jones see to their right that the track is mangled and misaligned after approximately ten feet. A rock slide from the collapsed section of the chamber caused this damage. Peering to their left, they noticed the track leading downward into darkness. Levi began investigating the wreck.

"That must be the way out of here. Help me lift this mine cart back onto the track."

"Are you crazy, Levi? This thing doesn't even look safe. Who knows where these tracks lead? It's pitch-black down there!"

"Do you have any other ideas? Because, last time I looked, the only way out is haunted by a ghost and destroyed by an earthquake."

Jones grunts while they attempt to lift the mine cart upright.

"You have a point. Come on, let's try to stand this thing upright."

After struggling and heaving, they finally re-positioned the rickety mine cart back onto the track. Levi suggests they hurry, get in the cart, and go.

"Wait!"

"What?"

Jones displays an embarrassed expression.

"I have to go to the bathroom."

"Well, go back into that room and go. I'll wait for you here."

Jones hesitantly returns to the eerie cave and looks for a place to relieve himself, eventually discovering a spot near the previously shifting pile of bones. While relieving himself against the rock wall, he mutters to himself.

"Don't look down. Don't look at the pile of bones."

In the middle of handling his business, he hears that eerie popping again and stares straight at the wall, instantly frightened as his eyes nearly pop out of his head. After zipping up and glancing over his shoulder, he is shocked to find that the skeleton has reassembled, its skull displaying an angry gesture. Jones yells and dashes toward the mine cart as the skeleton pursues him.

Meanwhile, Levi climbs into the mine cart and tries to figure out his next move when Jones' screams grab his attention from the distance. He is sweating heavily as he runs at full speed. It doesn't matter how fast Jones runs because the skeleton is right behind him and gaining. He turns the corner and yells at Levi.

"Go, Go, Go!"

Jones leaps into the air and lands in the mine cart before Levi can grasp what's happening. That force suffices to push it down the track. They both turn and look back, watching the skeleton fall into a pile of bones once more, just before the mine cart plunges downhill into the darkness. They both squat down and grip onto anything they can to keep themselves from being thrown out as they scream hysterically. The cart falls nearly vertically, creating a sensation of zero gravity. It travels along the rusty, crooked track, rolling over and under the mined-out path in the darkness, resembling a frightening, broken roller coaster ride. The runaway carriage speeds up, often teetering on just two wheels as it navigates corners.

The wheels grind and shoot sparks like firecrackers. As the mine cart advances, it navigates vast caverns filled with skeletons, shattered bones, crushed helmets, ore embedded in the rock walls, and mining machinery. The runaway ride quickly swings through the carved-out corridors. The mine cart races up, down, left, and right through endless cave tunnels until it reaches a section of the track that crests over a deep, open mine gorge, where it slows down. Halting entirely, it balances at the peak like a still teeter-totter. Levi peeks over the edge of the cart.

"Why did we stop?"

"I don't know. Is this ride over yet? I want to get out of this thing."

"We are stuck. We need to get out of here."

In the background, they hear sounds of water droplets and bat colonies. They don't realize that a slight lean forward would prolong this ride of horror. Jones panics.

"I'm scared. I want to get off this thing."

He then let out a loud sneeze, strong enough to jolt the cart forward. As they move over the peak, Levi yells at his adventurous companion.

"Jones! No!"

The cart speeds up, almost plunging off the track, as the two scream in terror. The sounds of grinding metal and hammering overshadow their cries for help. All at once, the metal bolts of the rusty transport begin to vibrate and come loose. Swarms of bats soar above them after each sharp turn. The jagged tunnel walls, lined with thick spiderwebs and roots, blur as they race by, gaining speed. Throughout this intense ride, the speed threw previous mine carts from the track.

They pass skeletons of deceased miners, who remain in their position, clutching their tools as if still engaged in mining, even in death. Just as the boys are about to lose their grip and tumble out of the vehicle, it enters a vast, eerie cavern illuminated in purple by underground lakes on either side of the track. The cart abruptly decelerates on the shaky bridge without coming to a complete stop. While Levi gazes through a crack in the rotting wood of the cart, the purple light glows brightly, illuminating submerged rock formations in the vast bodies of water. Since they would fall directly into the glowing water if they jumped out of the mine cart, they stay put. Oddly enough, the track is completely level, yet the cart continues to move forward slowly.

As they peer over the edge, they observe an increased number of broken crates and the remains of fallen miners. Levi is out of breath.

"This is insane! Where are we now?"

Jones' mouth hangs open.

"I don't have a clue. Look at all the dead people, Levi. There must have been hundreds of people working down here."

Levi closes his eyes for a moment.

"Please, please, don't come to life."

He reflects on the events that occurred at the start of this journey. Gigantic spiders dangle from their webs high above the track. On the bridge, which is scarcely constructed over varying levels of rock formations, the cart suddenly halts. The dilapidated bridge appears unable to bear any additional weight beyond what it currently supports. The chamber is completely silent, and the water remains still. Jones panics again.

"What are we supposed to do now?"

"I don't know, but if we don't get out of this thing, we'll end up..."

The instant bubbling of the water interrupts Levi. The water boils quickly, causing steam to rise from it. Jones trembles in place.

"You can't be serious."

The water continues to boil, filling the space with steam, and Levi quickly becomes anxious.

"I can't do this. We've gotta leave."

The boys shiver, scanning the rocky landscape anxiously for a solution. Near the mine cart, a green orb of light surfaces beneath the water's surface. In a slow and dramatic fashion, the ghost miner's image materializes, rising above the boiling water and hovering a few feet above them. He still wears an angry scowl, glaring at the boys.

"What's taking you so long?"

Jones believes the miner is blind, unaware of their predicament.

"We are stuck on this track! There is no way we can move."

The ghost becomes more aggravated by the second, then slowly descends back into the boiling water, disappearing under the cover of steam. Levi grows annoyed.

"What is his problem? What does he think we can do? We are stuck here?"

Shortly after Levi's statement, the water stops boiling, and silence falls upon the chamber once more. The boys settle back in, attempting to decide what to do next. Instantly, eerie popping noises interrupt their mumbling ideas to each other. With his eyes wide open, Jones grabs Levi's arm before peeking over the edge of the cart.

"Oh no! It can't be. Not again!"

Levi looks at Jones.

"What do you w…"

Levi is startled when he turns and sees what shocks Jones. Standing on the track and peering down at the boys is a huge, ghostly skeleton with glowing flames for eyes and an evil grin on its face. The eight-foot-tall skeleton's grimy bones glow a bright white, with sparks emanating from them, as each joint appears to be connected by some magical force. As the skeleton forcefully grabs and pushes the back of the mine cart, the boys scream. It remains behind the cart, pushing it uphill as its jaw hangs open. A loud, terrifying laugh emanates from the bony specter as it pushes itself so hard that its lower body struggles to keep up.

Screeching sounds and sparks erupt from the mine cart as it rolls over a rocky boulder. The ride grows rougher and more chaotic as they descend the shaky track. An approaching break in the railing is seen by the boys. The spooky specter pushes even faster, making the cart jump down the track before the break and land precisely where the rails continue. The experience grows increasingly perilous as the track twists and becomes uneven. Levi and Jones feel nauseous.

Levi is about to puke when he notices more bats flying toward them from every direction. Dodging diving bats and the sudden twist of the warped tracks, they desperately try to remain in the damaged cart. The ground vanishes as vast voids and open pits emerge beneath the rails. The track keeps twisting and turning as the cart wheels lose their grip and direction. Regrettably, the boys come to understand that the cart will not remain on the track for much longer. Levi screams in horror.

"Hold on! This thing is falling apart!"

Jones quietly watches the end of the track approach in the distance. The skeleton laughs even louder and refuses to slow down. After traversing a deep underground ravine, the skeleton immediately releases its grip. The boys turn around and watch as the bones collapse and fall into the gorge. As the track approaches its end, they swiftly shift their focus to the front of the terror ride.

"Oh no, Levi! Dead end coming! Duck!"

It didn't take long for them to crash into an old, dried-out rail car stop that shattered upon the impact of the mine cart. The impact threw them from the cart, and their arms and legs thrashed everywhere. With screams of horror, they both land in a massive pile of large feathers. Cracked wood, bent trim, and hardware litter the ground as pieces of the wooden cart lay shattered. A column of smoke ascends from the heated, exhausted wheels. Stunned by the fall, the boys attempt to collect themselves while sprawled on the thick pile of feathers that cushioned their landing. Still damp and dirty, they realize the escapade ripped some of their clothing.

A feeling of dread constantly lingers in the boys' minds as they gasp for air, coughing and brushing off the dust. Everywhere they have ventured so far is dark, and they often encounter a horrible surprise. They wonder where they are now, as this unfamiliar area differs from the others. A cool breeze flows as the surrounding phosphorescent rocks cast an eerie glow. Along this musty expanse are thick thatches of daddy long-leg spiders, webbing, and nesting material. There is no ceiling visible in this area; the higher the boys look, the darker and emptier it becomes. All they see behind them is darkness, as if everything before has simply vanished. Jones is in awe.

"Ugh, I hurt. Where are we now? How can there be wind blowing underground?"

"I don't know."

"Where are we supposed to go, Levi? If we had that map the crazy ol' miner guy was talking about, maybe we could find the treasure and go home."

Feeling around the vast bed of feathers, they sit while Levi questions everything.

"What is this that we landed on?"

Attempting to crawl off the pile, Jones answers his best buddy.

"Whatever it is, it sure smells."

Levi inspects the nest.

"Check out the size of these things."

Almost off the pile, Jones responds.

"I've never seen feathers like this before. But what has feathers this big?"

An abrupt, haunting shriek pierces the near silence in the darkness above, scaring the boys instantly. Levi tries to put logic over his fears.

"What is that?"

The shrieking generates a significant vibration as it grows increasingly louder. Jones, now on his feet, yells.

"I don't know what that is, but we need to run!"

The breeze intensifies as mammoth flapping and aerial floundering noises escalate in intensity. A pair of glowing, bloodshot eyes hovers above Levi's head.

"No, no, there is no way that can be what I'm thinking."

The shriek is extremely loud, and the eyes are drawing nearer. A massive, filthy, disfigured bird creature emerges from the darkness. This bird has a thick, solid beak, blood-soaked feathers, and scars from past fights. Like heavy hail falling from the sky, the bird keeps the boys in sight. Levi struggles to climb out of the feathery nest. Jones reaches for Levi's hand and pulls him from the nest. They dash into a nearby tunnel as the bird soars above them. Because the tunnel is narrow and not high enough for the bird to maneuver, tons of rocks and debris fall everywhere when its wings strike the sides. Jones screams as the bird pursues at full speed, destroying everything in its wake.

"Run, run, run!"

The wind generated by the bird's wings makes running difficult for the youngsters, as if they are trapped in a vacuum cyclone. Levi gazes into the distance and sees the tunnel's end coming closer.

"Jones! When I count to three, dive to the ground!"

"W... What?"

"One... Two... Three,"

They both instantly dive to the ground, landing on their bellies. The creature flies above them as soon as they land, colliding with the dead end, causing the rock wall to shatter and crumble. A dense cloud of dust and dirt fills the air as the explosion shook the ground. The boys observe another open area behind the damaged wall as the now ultra-disfigured creature vanishes into the darkness below.

"Jones! Jones! Are you okay?"

Jones sits up, shaking the dust and rock off his head. Before speaking, he spits pebbles and dirt out of his mouth.

"Ugh! Yeah, I guess so. What was that thing, Levi? How is it underground? Can you still see it?"

Levi looks around and notices the new entrance.

"I don't see anything. If that bird is down here, there must be an opening somewhere. It doesn't make sense. Something is not right. How can these things be real?"

As if watching a steam boiler explode under excessive pressure, Jones could no longer take it.

"Dang it! I can't deal with this anymore! Where is that miner? I would love to tell him off!"

"Calm down, buddy. Try to relax."

"No! It's not right! We don't deserve this. We didn't do anything, and now we are stuck down here! I want to go home, but we don't even know where to go or what we're doing. Where are you, miner? You did this to us! Come here now!"

Silence immediately fills the area. Levi is startled.

"Oh no. What did you do?"

A loud moan echoes throughout the tunnel instantly. Where the bird vanished, the new entrance glows green from below. A translucent green orb slowly floats from the depths and hovers above the boys. Jones is livid.

"I'm not afraid of you anymore! Why are you doing this to us? We don't know where to go or what we are looking for! I'm not moving another inch until you explain yourself."

For the first time in his life, he has no fear on his face. In front of Jones, the orb turns bright white, forcing both of them to shield their eyes. In a flash, the spectral miner appears with a heavy scowl still on his face and engages in a dead stare-down with Jones.

"Jones, backup!"

"No! He brought us here, and he's going to explain himself."

The miner leans forward, staring at Jones, his mouth dripping with black drool.

"How dare you question me! You want to know what's happening?"

He lifts his arm and snaps his fingers.

"I'll show you."

Bright flashes and crackling stars fall from the miner's hand, floating in Jones's direction.

Chapter 5

As he snaps his gnarled fingers, a radiant, soft blue flame erupts, dancing and flickering with an enchanting glow that lights up the surrounding darkness. The flame dances through the air, trailing a sparkling string of white embers as it glides gracefully toward Jones. Levi's eyes widened in disbelief as he witnessed the fire dancing in midair, as though it were burning on an invisible candle. Levi froze as Jones's eyes widened and teeth clenched while the blue flame engulfed him. Jones' body trembled and shivered involuntarily, his muscles twitching beneath his skin. Despite the translucent flame flickering ominously around him, he feels no heat; instead, he experiences significant discomfort. His hands are positioned at his sides, palms facing up, with fingers in a gripping shape. White sparks fall from his feet as he hovers above the ground. Brilliant blue orbs materialize and gently hover above his clawed hands, casting an otherworldly glow. The whites of his eyes gleam intensely, enhancing the eerie yet captivating aura surrounding him. Blurry waves move rhythmically around the flashing orbs. A steady, strong breeze is intensifying throughout the area. Levi shakes with fear.

"Oh, my gosh! What's happening?"

He watches in terror as his friend transforms.

"Jones! Jones! Wake up! Let him go ghost man."

The specter turns his head and stares menacingly at Levi.

"Quiet! Jones is eager to understand the situation, so I'm imprinting the map details and a few additional items into his subconscious."

Suspended a few feet off the ground, Jones gazes into the abyss with an unsettling intensity, as if a dark force has taken hold of him. He is deeply connected to the mine's history and its treasures through the miner's magical touch. A sudden wave of terror washes over him, causing his head to jerk wildly from side to side, his eyes wide with disbelief. Levi shouts at the ghost.

"What are you doing to him?"

"He's feeling how I died."

Jones lets out a blood-curdling scream as his body jerks and spasms uncontrollably! Levi helplessly watches his best friend suffer.

"Leave him alone!"

Jones's body slowly drops to the ground as the miner waves his hand. The flames that burn in his eyes return to the miners' hands. With the wind ceasing, Levi found Jones almost lifeless before him. The ghost stares at Levi.

"Now that he's aware of the map's contents, there's no time to waste! Begin the journey or face the consequences of inaction."

With a profound sigh, the miner gradually disappears into the earth. After he vanished, Levi kneels beside Jones, gently shaking him to rouse him from the moment.

"Wake up! Wake up!"

After lying still and seemingly lifeless for several seconds, Jones lets out a moan before finally waking up.

"W... what h... happened?"

Levi feels relieved but stammers.

"You were floating. You were floating and on fire... blue."

"W... what? Blue, what?"

Levi notices faint light blue flames flickering in Jones's eyes.

"What's wrong with your eyes?"

"What do you mean, what's wrong with my eyes? I've never seen clearer in my life."

"Jones, you have a fire in your eyes!"

"What? You're nuts!"

Levi then stares at a chain that appears around Jones's neck and at something glowing under his shirt.

"What's that?"

"What's what?"

Jones stands and looks down, gripping the chain and noticing the green glow from below his shirt. With a mighty tug on the chain, he uncovers a jaw-dropping revelation.

"It's a green jewel! One, like the miner, told us he had to wear."

Levi, feeling confused, asks a question.

"Where did it come from?"

Jones attempts to remove it, but he can't because the amulet's unusual power holds it around his neck.

"I can't take this thing off. Perhaps it will bring us luck, as it did for the miner. Although being stuck down here hasn't brought much luck. Ugh. Oh well, come on, we've got to go this way."

Jones gestures for Levi to follow him as he proceeds to the next area. Levi scratches his head.

"You're right. I doubt any luck can come from that thing. Wait, how do you know where you're going?"

"I don't know, I just have a suspicion."

Levi believes his friend is unusually calm and rational.

"Isn't he scared?"

Seemingly half-conscious, Jones invites Levi to follow him into the passage created by the bird creature.

"Are you OK?"

"I'm quite well, Levi."

After hearing Jones speak like this for the first time, Levi shakes his head in disbelief. He trails behind his best friend as they navigate over fallen boulders, rubble, and rocks. As they venture further into the new area, they encounter a formidable opening that gapes before them like the mouth of a giant. Sharp edges resembling jagged teeth glisten ominously in the near darkness. In the center of the underground gorge, a thin rope bridge spans across. Above them, all they can see is a pitch-black void.

They carefully descend the broken rock of the damaged passage to a platform anchoring one end of the bridge. Intricate hieroglyphs and mysterious writings adorn ancient artifacts scattered throughout the area. Various components of mining equipment encircle the platform, creating a rugged and industrious atmosphere. On both sides of the bridge, two sturdy bamboo poles rise, each supporting a torch that can hold fire. Feathers intricately bound with twine fuel these torches. The damp, metallic smell pervades the air.

Although the torches aren't lit, when Jones stares at them, the blue flame in his eyes ignites them. The fire provides bright illumination to the area. Jones pauses in front of the rope bridge before taking his first step onto it. In the distance, he glimpses another platform, its view obstructed by a towering rock wall marked by a series of meticulously chiseled holes. Ominously looming, the stone facade casts shadows over a weathered pedestal centered before it, guarding its secrets. The four large bamboo posts supporting the unstable rope platform seem likely to be unstable under pressure. The bridge is deteriorating, as shown by the dried vine and decaying bamboo flooring. Jones stares at the overpass, while Levi gazes at him, seemingly in a trance. Knowing that Jones has the map memorized, Levi questions him.

"Well, do we cross it?"

"Yes."

Levi extends his hand, showing the bridge.

"You first."

Jones places one foot at a time on the bamboo flooring. The bridge sways back and forth because of his slow movements. Levi's fear paralyzes him. Jones crosses the overpass slowly, as if unconsciously ignoring the bridge's deteriorating condition. Under pressure, the braided ropes pull and stretch. Levi feels relieved his friend reaches the bridge's center, as Jones focuses on the next platform.

"Careful, Jones!"

One foot in front of the other as the bridge sways, Jones finally makes it to the other end. He turns around and stares at Levi with a silent, blank grin, gesturing for him to cross.

"Your turn."

Levi places one foot on the bridge, revealing his nervousness. The rope tightening and the cracking bamboo post grow louder as he steps forward with his other foot. The old span sways gently while the torches crackle and flicker. Sweat beads form on Levi's forehead as he walks carefully across the platform, watching where he steps. Unlike Jones's journey, the bridge weakens with each step taken. A chilling howl emerges from the dark depths beneath Levi as he reaches the center of the overpass. He lets out a shriek as he looks down.

"What the?"

As a gust of wind bursts from the depths, he sees two bulging, bloodshot eyes. The moment the loud flapping sounds reach his ears, his thoughts become a whirlwind, making it hard to focus. The powerful gusts of wind surge from below, making the bridge sway from side to side. Levi feels the boards beneath his feet tremble as he hurriedly navigates the rickety planks. With each step, he can hear the creaking of the bridge, and a sense of urgency surges through him. He missteps in his panic; the bamboo flooring breaks. Levi struggles to cross the bridge while more bamboo splits. The grotesque howls grew louder, and the wind became nearly tornado-like. He talks to himself to keep going.

"No, No, No. Come on, Levi, you can do it."

Upon reaching the end of the bridge, he jumps onto the platform where Jones stands. He collapses to the ground in front of Jones as the menacing, vulture-like creature soars upward from the dark pit, crashing into the bridge and instantly demolishing it. The explosion and debris from the bridge cause Jones to fall backward while Levi shrieks hysterically. At the bridge's start, the creature put out the torches. The only light source comes from the bamboo torches next to the boys. Soaring back from the shadows, the fierce, winged creature swoops down again, determined to make a bold last effort against the two below. It nearly hits them, missing by only inches. Levi looks at Jones, who remains perfectly still and grinning while gazing straight ahead. Levi stammers.

"Did you... see the... bird... bridge?"

He understands there is no turning back after forcing himself to breathe slowly and steadily. They both stand up, dusting themselves off. Jones pivots on his heels, his gaze fixed on the wall adorned with intriguing shapes carved deep into its surface. Curiosity sparks in Levi's eyes as he quickly joins him, both captivated by the enigmatic artistry before them. With the intensity of blue fire blazing in his eyes, Jones unleashes a concentrated glare that lights the bamboo torches carefully mounted along the jagged surface of the rock wall. Each flame bursts to life, illuminating the surrounding darkness with warm, flickering light and sending playful shadows skittering across the rugged stone, creating an atmosphere thick with anticipation and mystery. Delicate spider webs glisten in the light, intricately woven between the twisting vines that cling to the rugged rock wall. The surface has five holes of different shapes carved into it. A hefty, flat rock serves as a makeshift table, balanced on top of two smaller stones that lift it two feet off the ground. On this table are five differently shaped stones that do not fit the openings in the wall. A shiny piece of broken metal that resembles a small antique hand mirror lay next to the rocks on the table. As Levi approaches the wall, he pushes the vines and webs aside.

"What is this? Is this a puzzle? I don't understand it."

Jones intervenes.

"This is how we continue our journey. We must fit the rocks into the correct hole and, when completed, something miraculous will happen."

"But how? The rocks don't match the shape of the holes."

"We must fit the rocks into the correct hole, and something miraculous will happen."

Levi looks down at the table.

"What is this shiny metal for?"

"We must fit the rocks into the correct hole, and something miraculous will happen."

Staring at the wall, Levi complains.

"I don't know what you mean!"

In his frustration, Levi picks up one of the rock puzzle pieces and attempts to fit it into one of the specifically shaped holes. "What did I tell you? It doesn't fit!"

Immediately after his statement, the ground trembles.

"Now what?"

Levi surveys the area as the ground shakes violently, causing a piece of the platform beneath them to collapse into the dark abyss. Suddenly, the tremors cease.
"I wouldn't put the wrong rock into the wrong hole again, or our journey will be over soon."

"What the heck is wrong with you? This is crazy, and you're so calm. What did that miner do to you?"

Jones stares at the puzzle for an extended period, which frustrates Levi and prompts him to pace back and forth. He throws a tantrum, knocking the metal off the platform, then falls to his knees in tears, weeping in distress.

"We will never get out of here. We are going to die."

He sits and weeps as he surveys his future tomb, catching a glimpse of the wall's reflection in the shiny piece of metal positioned upright.

"What the?"

Picking up the shiny implement and looking at the reflection of the wall, the shapes of the holes changed into those of the rocks on the platform.

"Jones, I got it! I got it!"

He jumps to his feet and carefully places the first stone into a slot while simultaneously looking at the metal. In the distance, two torches suddenly ignite, and a loud grinding noise fills the air. On the other side of the wall lies a shadowy pit, its depths obscured by darkness. From the edge of the abyss, the outlines of another bridge materialize.

"Jones, look over there."

Levi picks up a second stone and places it in the correct position according to the reflection of the wall on the metal. They hear another grinding noise and more of the bridge swings toward them. Jones' enthusiastic grin fades briefly as he cheers on his friend while solving the puzzle. Levi picks up another stone and finds a small coin underneath it, falling from the table and rolling off the platform. A heavy, round stone slab slowly rolls away from a small, dark hole in the nearby wall, revealing a hidden passage behind it.

At that moment, a swarm of bats erupted from the dark crevice, their leathery wings flapping furiously as they filled the air with a frantic screeching. The sudden rush knocks Levi off balance, sending him stumbling forward. In the chaos, his hand inadvertently presses the stone puzzle piece into the wrong slot, a mistake that changes everything. The ground shakes more violently than it did before. Jones and Levi brace themselves as another enormous chunk of the platform cracks and falls into the black pit. As the boys dodge bats swooping around them, they soon run out of room to stand. Fear nearly paralyzes Levi, yet the calm expression on Jones' face belies that fact.

"Let's continue."

As soon as the ground stops shaking, Levi slowly stands up and continues to solve the puzzle by placing the third and fourth stones.

"This is crazy! Careful Jones! We are running out of room. I'm assuming that when I insert all five rocks, the bridge will free us."

Almost across the pit, the bridge nearly connects to the remaining platform where the boys stand. Carefully, Levi picks up the fifth piece, but it slips from his hands and falls to the ground, breaking in two.

"Oh, no! Are you kidding me?"

To his great annoyance, he examines the bridge's length. He realizes it isn't close enough to the platform to jump on, so he must complete the puzzle. He scoops up the two shattered pieces with a determined grip, aligning them like puzzle parts. Taking a deep breath, he forces them into the right slot, hoping against hope that they will fit together once more. In an exhilarating heartbeat, the ground trembles beneath them as the bridge locks into place, sealing the connection with a dramatic flourish. Rocks and debris tumble from above, showering the boys as they cling to the rapidly eroding platform beneath their feet. The ground groans ominously as cracks spiderweb across the surface, threatening to give way entirely. With each tremor, splintered pieces of stone fall away into the abyss below, intensifying their sense of urgency and fear. Levi clutches Jones by the arm and pulls him across the bridge, using all his strength.

"Run!"

As they approach the middle of the bridge, enormous boulders fall. The sound of destruction defines the moment, obliterating what remains of the puzzle platform and sending it crashing into the black pit below. The ground trembles as massive stones crash down, dismantling the new bridge section by section.

"Come on, Jones, run!"

As they take their last step off the bridge, massive boulders fall from the darkness above, landing on the bridge and destroying what remains. The violent shaking of the ground causes them to stumble forward, but it soon comes to a stop. Levi yells in pain. Standing back up, the boys stare at the dark pit and the space where the bridge once stood. Jones, in his mysterious calmness, presses on.

"That was close. We must continue."

"We almost died! Aren't you scared?"

"Very much so."

Jones turns around, followed by Levi, only to see their next challenge, causing Levi's frustration to grow.

"Oh, come on! When is this going to end? What is this thing?"

The imposing frame of the entryway, crafted from massive, rugged stone slabs, looms ahead of the boys; its ancient charm and solid presence deter them from venturing into the unknown. Torches mounted next to the entrance flicker to life, illuminating the surrounding area with a soft glow. Just beyond the shallow entrance, two tunnels follow. Both passages are circular and have scars from pitchforks embedded in them. One tunnel beckons to the left, inviting them into its depths, while the other leads to the right, promising new discoveries. A small stack of broken wooden boxes and barrels lies between the two pathways. Perched on top is a partially dressed skeleton wearing a miner's hat. Shrouded in cobwebs, the eerie skull boasts a snake slithering menacingly from its eye socket, adding a spine-chilling touch to the haunted atmosphere. Based on the position of the remains, this corpse shared the same fate as the miners who came before him. Levi gagged as he focused on the gruesome sight before him.

"Oh, gross. That is disgusting."

Barrels atop the pile elevate the bony left arm, while his right hand appears to point to the right. The left hand holds an extinguished bamboo torch. Levi looks to Jones for answers.

"Wow, this is horrible. Which way do we choose?"

Jones gazes at the pile of bones for a moment.

"This is a perplexing predicament."

"Perplexing? Predicament? Since when do you talk like that?"

Jones stays silent while Levi shakes his head.

"Well, this guy seems to point to the right tunnel, so let's try it."

Then, the torch in the skeleton's hand ignited, casting a strange flickering light. Although frightened by the corpse, Levi hesitated to grab the torch. Gradually, they walk down the right tunnel. Thick wooden columns support the jagged walls of the tunnel, preventing the ceiling from caving in. Broken clay pots, partially mined ore, and various colored minerals litter the tunnel. A mangled mine cart track leads to nowhere in the middle of the corridor. The atmosphere is eerily quiet, with no sign of bats, rats, or other creatures to disturb the adventurers. To light the way, Levi holds the torch high in the air.

"There is something up ahead, but I can't make out what it is."

The dark tunnel is challenging to traverse, even with a torch. Almost halfway down the shaft, the boys hear something fall behind them, and they both turn to see what it is. Levi can barely hold the torch, trembling from fear.

"What was that?"

Out of nowhere, a crackling, sizzling sound erupts, growing louder. A composed Jones surveys the area.

"Do you smell something?"

"Yes, I do. But what is it?"

They glance ahead and realize that Levi accidentally lit something dangling from the top of the tunnel.

"Oh, no! What did I do?"

Looking further down the tunnel, they identify many red wooden boxes with white letters that read TNT. Levi screams at the top of his lungs.

"Oh no! I think I... I think I lit a fuse! Run!"

With a swift motion, he lets go of the torch, seizes Jones's arm, and drags him towards the entrance. The fuse burns rapidly, creating a dense smoke as it approaches the TNT. The boys sprint at full speed to escape the tunnel. With only a few feet of fuse left to burn, they return to the entrance and dash into the other tunnel. The TNT detonates with immense power, causing the ground to tremble as it propels bones, rocks, and ash out of the tunnel on the right. The explosion is powerful, causing the right tunnel entrance to collapse violently. After entering the left tunnel, the teens fell to the ground, covered in dust, ore, and small stones.

"Holy cow, did you see that, Jones? We almost died again, and there is no way we can go back now. Are you all right?"

"I think so. I think so. That was unexpected. We must continue."

"What are you? That was so scary. Didn't you hear what I said? We almost died again. You're acting like a robot or something."

"I'm just fine, Levi. We must continue. This way. This way, Levi."

Levi took a moment to stare at Jones, shaking his head in amazement. He stands up, dusts himself off, and then continues.

Chapter 6

Ancient, extinguished torches line the left tunnel, their char-coal-blackened ends a testament to a time when flame once il-luminated the passage. Levi and Jones continue walking forward despite the darkness and gloom of the tunnel. Upon Jones's approach to a lantern, the blue flame in his eye sparks the torch, casting light on the surroundings. Sharp, glowing chunks of crystallized ore jut out from the shaft's walls. The passage is lengthy, cumbersome, and takes a considerable amount of time to traverse. Despite the uneven and deteriorating ground, they navigated their way over large stones and fallen support beams.

As they move through this area, Levi remains worried, con-tinually on the lookout for any unexpected dangers. The zom-bie-like Jones keeps a calm demeanor. Levi feels relieved when they reach the end of the spooky passage encountering no other risks. They soon arrived in an ancient corridor. A collection of timeworn mining tools lies haphazardly across the ground, their rusted metal and worn wooden handles telling stories of count-less days spent in toil. In the vicinity, lean bamboo spears rest against the ancient rocks, their tips remaining sharp despite the passage of time. Scattered around them are pieces of sturdy armor, aged and battered, once worn to protect against fierce battles. Ancient animal-skin shields, frayed at the edges and adorned with faded markings, rest in a rugged pile, remnants of a bygone era rich with tales of survival and struggle. Roots and jungle-like vines obscure the fifteen-foot-high triangular frame of an unfamiliar door. Painstakingly carved into the stone frame are hieroglyphics. Three faces protruding from the bronze-colored metal door impede their progress. As they approach this new entrance, the torches behind them simultaneously blow out, and two torches mounted on the triangular entry ignite. Levi crouches and lifts a vibrant, weathered mask crafted from ancient decaying wood.

"What is this?"

As Jones surveys the scene, he appears at peace, wearing a goofy grin on his face. Levi thought out loud.

"I remember in history class seeing stuff like this. It almost resembles Aztec-type things."

He continues trying to break Jones out of his daydreaming state.

"Jones! Hello! Are you all there?"

Jones casts a glance at Levi, a mischievous grin playing on his lips.

"We need to continue."

Levi points to the large door adorned with detailed hieroglyphics carved into it.

"How are we supposed to continue?"

Jones notices unusual words beneath each of the three faces on the door.

"This is another puzzle."

Levi feels confused and increasingly frustrated.

"What do those words say?"

A sudden flash of brilliant green light erupts from the amulet hanging around Jones' neck. As he stares at the words on the door, the flames in his eyes grow brighter. A green spot shines on the ground behind the boys as an eerie, low moan echoes throughout the space. Levi's heart races with fear as he remembers that spine-chilling moan. Slipping stealthily behind Jones, he braces himself for the impending visit of the dreaded miner. Levi's eyes lock onto the apparition forming before him. Jones nonchalantly fixes his gaze on the doorway as if nothing out of the ordinary is happening. In the bright green energy, sand and stones swirl counterclockwise while a monstrous figure hovers above the ground. He rises from the ground, wearing an angry expression. The foul-looking specter glares at Levi.

"I'm surprised you have made it this far. I have never delved this deeply into the mine."

His mouth erupts with mucus froth, fueled by the thrill of excitement.

"As we approach the treasure, I can feel its power growing stronger. Time is of the essence. Complete your quest swiftly or face a dire fate."

Levi thinks something is wrong as he looks over Jones's shoulder.

"We're stuck and we can't open this door."

"Silence! I have put everything Jones needs to know in his mind. Figure it out or die!"

A chilling laugh echoes from the ghostly prospector before he vanishes back into the earth. The dirt and stones halt, and the green spot gradually fades away. Levi stops crouching behind Jones and stands where the ghost appeared.

"I don't understand. Why doesn't he realize we do not understand?"

"I've got it!"

Levi turns around with a surprised look on his face.

"You do?"

"Yes."

Jones points to the words beneath the three faces. He speaks in tongues as if he understands the inscriptions.

"Alob candorfious anatolta vindenio deulum,"

Inching closer to the door and looking at Jones, perplexed, Levi questions the moment.

"What does that mean?"

"In layman's terms, it says cover the prosperous, but beware."

A look of utter confusion appears on Levi's face as he glances at Jones.

"Cover the prosperous? Beware? What does that mean, and how do we do it?"

Jones spots the colorful, cracked mask that Levi is holding and grabs it.

"That is it! We need to place this mask over the face that is prosperous!"

"Huh? Say what? OK, but what does beware mean?"

Jones steps up to the front of the door. Three faces are sticking out of the door, each with a distinct expression. The first face radiates happiness with a bright, smiling face. The second face is shedding tears, while the third looks perplexed and unsure. A bracket secures each mask in place. Levi is becoming increasingly impatient as he wants to leave before anything else occurs. He snatches the mask back from Jones' hand.

"Well, it's obvious that this guy is smiling because he is prosperous."

Levi places the mask on the smiley face, and immediately, the ground shakes violently. Debris and rocks fall everywhere, and massive boulders soon collapse over the tunnel entrance. The shaft is completely obliterated, providing no means of escape. Boulders crash down toward the boys as they cling to the door. The shaking stops as the last boulder falls just feet away from them. Stress and panic overwhelm Levi.

"We are going to die!"

Jones calmly looks at Levi.

"Why did you grab the mask from my hands? I think I have it figured out."

"Why are you so calm? We were almost crushed. We're gonna die! We need to get out of here!"

"Stay calm, my dear friend. We will make it out of here. Unfortunately, you put the mask on the wrong face, and I fear another such mistake will end our journey here."

Astonished by Jones's jargon, Levi stares at him in wonderment.

"What's wrong with you, Jones?"

Jones looks up and sees two enormous boulders hanging directly above them; if they fall, the boys will be crushed.

"I am fine. Let's figure out this puzzle, Levi."

Jones stands before the door and takes the mask.

"Cover the prosperous."

He examines each face, lost in thought.

"Why would a man who is prosperous look confused? A prosperous man would be so happy that he would be crying."

With that, Jones gently places the wooden mask on the face of the crying person. Instantly, stones and debris tumble down, accompanied by a tremor that shakes the ground beneath. The massive bronze door slowly slides open. Jones picks up a torch and smiles at Levi. Impressed by his friend's deduction skills, Levi takes a deep breath and walks through the door. The air in this passage feels thick and clammy, saturated with humidity that lingers in the atmosphere, giving off a distinct, earthy odor reminiscent of damp wood and decaying leaves. Thick vines and lush green foliage drape gracefully over the ceiling and cascade down the walls, creating a verdant tapestry that seems alive. Droplets of water drip from everything. The scene amazes Levi.

"How can this be? Plants like these can't live underground, can they?"

As the thick foliage envelopes them, the two intrepid explorers remain oblivious to the multitude of sharp, observant eyes tracking their every move. White, round, dull sacs, like eggs, dot this area. Jones's expression shifts, a gravity settling over him that captures Levi's attention.

"Something isn't right."

"What do you mean?"

"This is way too easy. I know where we are heading, but it shouldn't be this easy."

"Why would you wish for more terrible stuff to happen? We almost died several times, and you're complaining? I'll take a simple way out any day over."

The sound of conga drums beating in a melodic rhythm disrupts him. A mix of surprise and fear spreads across Levi's face. Jones smiles.

"I thought so."

A series of torches ignite one by one behind the vines in unison with the drumbeats. The two now understand that this tunnel stretches for what seems like forever, and navigating its depths will be a real challenge. The drumbeats ahead catch their attention. Levi displays his frustration once again.

"No, no, no, no, come on!"

"We need to continue quickly, Levi."

They continue deeper into the passage, carefully avoiding the roots and vines that are intertwined with the ground. As Levi focuses on the frightening eyes of the creatures staring at them, the drumbeats grow louder. He places his hand on Jones's shoulder.

"Holy cow, do you see those eyes?"

Jones is in a trance-like state and is not aware of the creatures lurking around him. Instead, he concentrates on the end of the tunnel. The deep, resonant rhythm of drumbeats, which sets the atmosphere for the ceremonial or spiritual experience, starts native chanting. Levi surveys everything profusely.

"Where are those voices coming from?"

Jones does not have an answer. As they tread the jungle-themed path, the cacophony of chanting and drumbeats grows more intense with each step. Their senses intensify as a multitude of tiny spiders emerge from their hiding places in the ground and ascend the twisting vines. To avoid tripping, they carefully step over the many obstacles scattered along the path. Suddenly, the drumbeats and chants rise to a fever pitch. Jones and Levi exchange a tense glance and come to a halt. Jones tries to figure out what is going on.

"I wonder why those sounds are speeding up?"

Levi is trembling, and his nerves are almost shot.

"I'm afraid to go on."

Without warning, the drumming and chanting come to an abrupt halt. Levi is on the verge of experiencing a panic attack.

"Uh oh, W... W... what's happening now?"

"I'm not sure."

Other than the crackling of the torches, the tunnel is entirely silent. With every gaze fixed upon them, the boys stood in silence. A symphony of hissing sounds suddenly shatters the silence, accompanied by the skittering of tiny feet darting in the shadows. Levi is sweating profusely from nerves.

"Jeez. Now what?"

The scurrying and hissing sounds grow louder. Under their feet, the ground trembles as creepy crawlies move through hidden cracks and holes in the tunnel. Bats, rats, spiders, and other pests quickly fill the tunnel. Amid the chaos, Levi doesn't move a muscle.

"What are they doing?"

"I think they are running away."

"Running away from what?"

A palpable tension hangs in the air as the hissing and scuttling grow increasingly louder, hinting at the approach of something massive and ominous. The drumming and chanting begin once more. Suddenly, all the torches blow out. Something large approaches them, and Levi closes his eyes in fear as the boys drop to their knees. The entire experience feels surreal, like being in a haunted house that is malfunctioning. In a passing second, everything is silent. At the far end of the tunnel, torches relight one by one. Eventually, the last torch lights next to poor Levi and Jones. Jones stands up first, then Levi.

"I don't understand what is happening. All this craziness, and for what?"

Hundreds of footsteps stop instantly when they hear a powerful hiss. Simultaneously, they turn around and look behind themselves. Levi's jaw drops to the ground. Three feet behind them is a gigantic, puss-filled, mutated millipede monster staring at them. It makes a loud chik chik hiss noise. Jones grins meditatively while Levi screams, struggling to find his footing to run.

"Jones, run!"

The enormous annelid trails the boys with intense fervor, its colossal, glistening body emerging steadily from a gaping hole in the ceiling. As it unfurls, the writhing creature's segments ripple and sway, revealing a slick, iridescent surface catching the light. The boys glance back in a mix of fear and fascination, their hearts racing as they sense the creature's relentless pursuit. The atmosphere is thick with tension, amplifying the urgency of their escape. This creature measures forty feet and fills the passageway. Its legs scraping against the tunnel is deafening. As the boys run deeper into the tunnel, the drums and chanting resume and speed up. While the subterranean beast pursues them, it unleashes toxic substances from its pores. They sprint at full speed while Jones appears lost in thought, and Levi lets out a piercing scream.

"Keep going, Jones!"

Jones looks down, watching his amulet glow and intensify by the second.

"I wonder what that means?"

Advancing slowly, the monstrous millipede-like beast oozes poison from its grotesque fangs. The drumbeats and chants maintain a feverish, heart-pounding rhythm. A strange-looking wall ahead shows they are nearing the end of the tunnel.

"Jones! T... t... tunnel. We are running out of it!"

"That is a problem."

The vines glow with an electric green energy as the amulet flashes brightly. The tunnel is nearing its end as moans erupt. Levi continues to scream.

"There's no more tunnel!"

In an electrifying moment, a vertical circle abruptly appears between the boys and the beast, with the vines and amulet shimmering in bursts of light and sound. They have mere inches to spare as the creature draws nearer. With about fifty feet left before they reach a dead-end wall, Levi and Jones make a desperate leap just as the vertical circle transforms into a blazing wall of firework sparks. The tunnel's end looms just ahead as they hit the ground. The monstrous beast crashes into the shimmering barrier, letting out one final, spine-chilling howl before bursting into countless brilliant stars and sparks. Silence envelops them once more. The boys lie on their stomachs, spread out on the ground before the dead end.

"Jeez, are you OK, Jones? That was extreme!"

Jones gazes at his shirt in a state of bewilderment, barely uttering a word. The fiery barrier vanishes as quickly as it appeared. His amulet shines brightly, its power vibrating through the air. Suddenly, a small green orb materializes on the ground behind them, spinning rapidly. The swirling energy resurrected the miner. His gaze fixed upon the boys with an intense scowl. His anger remains unwavering, a menacing presence among the dust and stones.

"I can't join you in a physical form because this mine and caves have cursed me. I can follow you with the power of the amulet. Wherever you go, I can follow you and we can search for the treasure together. The amulet will protect you while on your quest. Keep going or die!"

In a state of panic, the boys shift their focus towards the looming dead-end wall before them. The wall's surface is rugged and weathered, hinting at decades, if not centuries, of neglect. Prominently featured in its center is a sturdy wooden lever, its dark surface polished by the hands of those who had come before them. Surrounding the lever are intricate hieroglyphic carvings of men with spears dancing around a fire in the center of the wall just above the lever. Vines and dense spider webs partially obscure the ancient writings. Jones clears some obstructions to focus on the carvings, while Levi tries to understand them.

"What does it all mean?"

"I'm not sure about the pictures, but I know we need to pull this lever to continue."

The miner's scowl gradually shifts into a sinister grin, revealing his jagged, hollowed cheeks. Wisps of ghostly mist swirl around him, enhancing his spectral form. With his bony fingers delicately intertwined, he taps them together in a slow, deliberate rhythm, each echoing sound adding to the eerie atmosphere. Shadows dance around him as the dim light flickers, highlighting the unsettling gleam in his hollow eyes.

"Yes, pull the lever and retrieve the treasure."

He lifts his arms and gently sinks back into the earth. Levi is confused.

"Is it me, or is he getting scarier?"

Jones mumbles as he focuses on the wall.

"We need to pull this lever to continue."

A cacophony of whirling noises fills the air as Jones grips the lever tightly, his muscles straining with the effort. The old, thick rope, frayed in spots and coated in years of dust, winds around aged pulleys and heavy counterweights, creaking as they move. With a slow, deliberate pull, he feels the tension in the rope before the rock wall rises, grinding against stone as it lifts into the dimly lit cavern above. As the dust settles, they see a dark new entrance. The unknown stretches before them, full of promises and perils, leaving them uncertain of what lies beyond this new-found threshold.

Chapter 7

Levi and Jones stand transfixed at the threshold of the newly opened entrance, their eyes wide with anticipation as they peer into the unknown that lies beyond. On the other side of the entryway lies a narrow tunnel, its damp walls cloaked in shadows. As the boys step inside, a heavy, musty scent that lingers in the warm air greets them, enveloping them like a thick blanket. The heat radiates from the stone surfaces, making the passage feel even more oppressive. The air is thick with stifling humidity, making every movement feel like a struggle for the boys. They shuffle and stagger, sweating under the weight of the sweltering heat, each step challenging against the heavy air clinging to their skin. The landscape is a haunting tableau, strewn with the remnants of a forgotten era—skeletons lie in silent testimony, while rusted pitchforks and worn tools hint at the toil that once filled these grounds. Patches of glimmering iron ore catch the light, adding an eerie beauty to this desolate scene. Levi complains as he and Jones turn the corner from the newly discovered entrance.

"Wow. It's hot down here. Give me a minute. I have to pee."

The moment he finds a place to relieve himself, he becomes worried about the bones lying on the ground because he recalls what happened to Jones after relieving himself next to a pile of bones. Lost in thought, Jones gazes intently ahead, watching the path unfold before them as he waits for Levi to return. Soon, Levi rejoins his friend, and they continue their journey. As the tunnel gradually widens, it opens into a breathtaking cavern. The air is thick with heat and the scent of sulfur. Narrowing, the path winds precariously between huge, glowing pools of molten lava that bubble and hiss, casting a flickering orange glow across the rocky walls. High above the ground, several towering spouts erupt with a dramatic display, sending forth sheets of boiling, bubbling, and smoking slag. The molten material cascades through the air like fiery waterfalls, creating a mesmerizing yet hazardous spectacle. The path narrows as they venture deeper into this sweltering oven. Jones strides forward with confidence.

"I think we should walk in this direction."

"What? Are you kidding me, Jones? It's like an oven in here. We will burn up in here. There's got to be another way."

"No, this is indeed the way."

He walks on as if no dangers are present. Levi reluctantly follows.

"This is ridiculous."

As dense plumes of smoke spiral upward, a cascade of molten slag bubbles and pools on either side of the winding path. The air is thick with the caustic scent of minerals and fire. Amidst it all, the relentless roar of flowing flames reverberates like thunder, echoing through the cavern.

"Jones, stop. This is dangerous."

Jones continues to walk in a trance-like state, sweating profusely and remaining silent. A colossal explosion bursts high above, shattering the haunting sound of bubbling lava and sending shock waves through the air. Levi screams when he spots a massive chunk of rock plummeting behind them.

"Oh no, run, Jones!"

The path behind them vanishes beneath a flow of molten lava. As Jones runs toward the end of the path, he signals for Levi to follow him. An ancient mine elevator looms at the end of the path, its worn wooden frame propped precariously between towering, weathered pillars. Sturdy, rough-hewn logs form the columns; thick, coarse twine rope expertly binds them together, creating a rustic yet solid structure. The ground trembles as lava and boiling slag incinerate everything behind the two. At last, they arrive at the elevator, its surface enshrouded in thick, tangled spider webs. Even more haunting is the collection of animal skulls hiding beneath the webbing. They jump onto the platform, and Levi panics.

"Up! Up! How do we make it go up?"

"I think pulling this lever would help."

The lava is now perilously close to the elevator, just mere feet away.

"Pull it now! Jones, snap out of it and pull the lever!"

Jones grips the weathered, brittle wooden lever and yanks it down with effort, setting a powerful mechanism into motion.

Suddenly, a massive boulder—a heavy counterweight—plummets to the ground on the left side of the platform, creating a thunderous crash that echoes through the chamber. Meanwhile, the elevator groans and creaks, its ancient ropes straining as it gradually ascends, inching upward. The lava is flowing faster than the elevator is moving. After it reaches five feet in the air, the timber columns ignite from the flow. As the floor rises slowly, Levi notices the dry timbers burning rapidly and becomes even more horrified.

"Faster, faster! Does this thing move any faster?"

"No."

Although the elevator has only a few feet left to ascend, the relentless blaze quickly consumes the timber columns, sending glowing embers swirling upward as it races toward the platform. Before long, the flames surge toward the moving platform, licking at its edges with fierce intensity. A thick, acrid smoke billows up from the floor as it ignites, causing them to jump to higher ground. They crawl from the cliff's edge and watch flames consume the elevator. It blazes a fierce red, and Levi stands frozen in fear as everything plunges into the molten lava. Jones stares blankly into the air as if nothing ever happened, while Levi weeps with relief. Levi lunges at Jones, his palm connecting sharply against Jones's cheek repeatedly, each slap ringing like thunder in the tense atmosphere.

"Wake up, wake up, wake up!"

After one last mighty slap, the vibrant blue flame within Jones's eyes explodes, propelling them apart in a dazzling burst.

They land several feet apart, sitting on their rear ends. Levi feels dazed.

"Ugh! What happened?"

He crawls over to Jones, who appears asleep, and shakes him.

"Are you there? Jones! Jones!"

He abruptly opens his eyes, coughing as he brushes off the dust.

"Why did you hit me? What's going on? Where are we?"

"You're back!"

"Back from what? All I remember was being furious with that miner. Then everything went black."

"It seemed like you were under some spell. The Miner mentioned he filled your mind with all sorts of information. You were acting crazy because when we faced serious dangers. You just had this stupid grin on your face!"

"Hey! Hey! Hey! I'm not insulting you! I don't have a stupid…"

Jones is silenced by a loud vibrating moan. A thick, eerie green fog suddenly blankets the ground, swirling and billowing as if alive. A shadowy figure rises from within its depths, suspended in the air. It's the Miner. With an intense fury simmering just beneath the surface, the Miner looms before the boys, his expression a storm of indignation. He jabs a finger toward Jones, his eyes blazing with anger and disappointment, emphasizing the weight of his words as he prepares to confront him.

"My patience is running out. You may be out of the trance, but still know the treasure's location. I need that treasure. Find it! Now!"

The amulets around Jones' and the miners' necks pulsate in unison. The old prospector seems more agitated and can't stay still—his expression shifts between anger and dissatisfaction. Levi stands up for his friend.

"We are trying. We've almost died several times looking for it. This mine is horrible. We want to go home."

"Silence! You are getting closer. I can feel it."

With discontent etched deeply in his brows, Jones fixes a piercing glare upon the Miner.

"Come on, Levi. Let's keep going."

The ghoul laughs.

"Retrieve it or stay here forever!"

He gradually descends back into the earth as if cradled by the soil beneath him. Levi's gaze sharpens as he observes a flicker of blue flames rekindling in Jones' eyes. While he is gathering his bearings, Levi continues to pull his arm.

"Where do we go now?"

"I think we should go this way."

With that, they continue walking for a short while. Levi grows impatient.

"Is that a light ahead?"

"I think it is."

Levi gets excited when he notices an opening leading outdoors.

"Look, it's daylight. Let's go."

As the boys sprint towards the opening at the end of the dark tunnel, a sense of anticipation fills the air. With each step, the cool, damp air from the passageway gives way to a warmer breeze that brushes against their skin. Finally, they burst through the archway and a breathtaking vista greets them. Standing atop a rugged mountain peak, they gaze in awe at the expansive landscape unfolding before them. An entrance to another shaft is on the other side of the forty-foot-long cliff. The boys lean over the cliff's rugged edge, their eyes widening with wonder at the scene unfolding beneath them. Through the leaves of small trees, the sun filters, casting dappled shadows on the ground below. The vibrant greens and browns of the forest created a stunning tapestry. They spot rabbits darting playfully through the underbrush, their fluffy tails bobbing as they scamper away. A family of deer grazes peacefully nearby, their ears twitching at the slightest sound. Another mangled mine track leads into the other entrance. Levi feels frustrated because there is no simple way to exit this area.

"There is no way down from here."

"I estimate it's about one hundred feet down to ground level."

Both boys notice that this outdoor space resembles nothing they have ever seen in their town.

"We have to go back into the mine, Levi."

"What? Oh man, this is unbelievable! We are finally outside, and you want to go back in there?"

Jones glances at Levi and nods his head. As they approach the new mine shaft entrance, something seems different. A thick haze of steam-like vapor clings to the ground, swirling ominously and creating an eerie, otherworldly atmosphere. Jones looks back at Levi, not realizing that the translucent blue flames in his eyes intensified.

"I think we are getting close."

"Jones, the flame in your eyes is getting brighter."

"Let's do this."

As the boys enter the entrance, the sunlight fades, giving way to a shadowy atmosphere enveloped in deepening dark- ness. All they see are dark, hazy, dirty, dingy shadows. Columnar tree trunks and cracked beams placed every six feet help sup- port the area from collapsing. Old, worn lanterns, unlit for over a century because of lack of fuel, decorate each beam. In the distance, they hear steam being released under pressure. Every ten feet, robust galvanized pipes protrude from the wall, their metallic surfaces gleaming under the overhead lanterns.

Each pipe stretches outward before gracefully curving back toward the wall, creating a rhythmic pattern that draws the eye along the length of the corridor. Steam is leaking from various points. Pipes drip a luminous blue liquid, cascading onto the floor and meandering through the tunnel, providing the sole light source in the dark depths. Along this passageway, an eerie sight presents itself: several rusting mine cars, their metallic bodies marred by age and decay. Turned on their sides, they lie askew, covered in grime, and surrounded by the lingering scent of damp earth. A mine cart track runs down the center of the tunnel. Whenever the mine track comes into contact with the blue fluid, it vanishes as if being eaten by acid. Levi cautions Jones.

"Look at that blue liquid. See what it's doing to the tracks? Don't step in it."

"I have no intention of touching it."

As they venture deeper into the earth, bats swooping past or terrifying spiders staring at them startle the boys.

"I'm getting nervous, Jones. Don't you remember what happened the last time we were in a dark mine shaft?"

Jones doesn't respond.

"Jones! Did you hear what I asked you?"

Jones halts abruptly and turns back to Levi, remaining silent. The intense blue flames in his eyes make it hard for Levi to see his pupils.

"We are very close to the Shard of Chance. We must keep going."

"Shard of Chance? What is a Shard of Chance? Jones! Jones!"

The delicate streams of vibrant blue fluid weave through the uneven ground, creating varying-sized puddles. Some small pools are so expansive that the boys must make an agile leap to avoid splashing into them. When Levi jumps over a giant puddle, the heel of his shoe inadvertently contacts the liquid, causing it to smoke and nearly melt. He falls to the ground, yelling as he removes his shoe to inspect it.

"Jeez! Wow. My shoe."

Once the shoe stopped smoking, he put it back on. Jones moves forward.

"We must hurry."

The boys finally arrive at an immense, circular cavern, its towering dome arched high above them like the ceiling of a grand cathedral. As they cross the threshold into this expansive space, the mesmerizing blue fluid that has been their guide abruptly halts, pooling at their feet. At that moment, astonishment struck the boys silently, their eyes wide as they take in the breathtaking sight.

Chapter 8

A beautiful layer of white sand blankets the cave floor, sparkling gently in the soft glow of the blue ooze. Spider webs decorate every corner, shimmering like magical threads crafted by nature. Every web captures the faintest glimmers of light, creating a captivating, almost dreamlike atmosphere in this enchanting space. Levi and Jones stand roughly fifty feet from a colossal boulder, its rugged surface jutting out from the sand, partially submerged. The heart of this boulder features a striking elongated shard of deep blue, radiating an almost ethereal glow that captures the eye and draws the attention. The cave, illuminated by the shard, emits a low pulsating bass sound. Jones grabs Levi as he approaches the mysterious fragment.

"No! Don't walk towards it. Something is not right. It's too easy and danger lurks ahead."

"What do you mean by saying something is not right? Let's go investigate that thing."

Levi steps on the sand to investigate the shard, and his footprint sinks into nothingness. Blue fluid fills the void where he stepped, flowing under the sand like a river. Jones yanks him back while still holding him.

"I told you something isn't right. Don't walk on the sand!"

"Where the… what the… where's the sand…. my shoe. This fluid ate it."

"Don't move!"

A swirling green mist rises from the sand behind them, twisting and curling like a living entity. Slowly, it coalesced into the unmistakable shape of the Miner. As the figure of the apparition becomes almost complete, both boys turn to look at the Miner's scowl and rage. The ghost's amulet glows even brighter as it spins on the chain around his neck.

"You're so close. Can you sense its power?"

Noticing the blue shard, he moves closer. He wants to touch the fragment, so he extends his hands above it. Hovering between his twisted fingers and the shard are tiny white sparks.

"Yes, you're very close. I can almost grasp it. What's taking you so long? You must figure out how to retrieve the treasure. I can feel its power. The end is near! You must figure out how to touch this shard to continue. Its power is glorious. It grows stronger the closer we are."

Levi is tiring of the miners' threats.

"We can't walk across this sand. It breaks apart and turns into that blue goop that almost ate my shoe."

"That is not my problem. You accepted the quest and must figure out how to secure the treasure. Time grows short, hurry or suffer the consequences!"

With that final warning echoing in the air, the Miner becomes engulfed in a swirling mist, his form dissipating and sinking into the earth as if he had never existed. Levi turns to Jones, a mixture of concern and curiosity across his face.

"Now, what are we supposed to do? I want to go home. We are stuck in this mess, and I..."

Jones raised his hand to Levi's face, silencing him.

"This is just another puzzle we need to figure out. We can't walk across the sand because we will sink in that blue muck. The shard is too far away for us to jump on it. Hmmm."

They sit cross-legged at the edge of the unsettling sand. Levi clenches his hands, cradling his cheeks, while Jones meditates, attempting to find a solution.
"I don't understand it. If we walk on the sand, we'll sink and this blue stuff will eat us, but we must reach that crystal thing to escape. I just don't know how we are gonna do that."

Still, in a meditative state with blue flames flickering in his eyes, Jones thinks out loud.

"I'm not sure either. I'll figure it out."

Levi runs through many ideas in his head.

"Well, we have nothing to build a bridge or something to walk on to get to that shard."

Jones' eyes opened wide.

"Wait, that's it! We need to travel across something to get to the shard."

"Ah, that's what I just said, but how? Jones! Are you in the same place as me? How can we make something out of nothing? There's only sand, spiders, and this blue goop."

A shiver courses through Jones's body as his eyes roll back, a fleeting moment where time seems to stand still. The blue flames in his eyes grow brighter, matching the bubbling blue sludge as it boils.

The emerald-green amulet hanging from his neck radiates a soft, enchanting light, casting a gentle glow that dances across his skin. His mouth hangs agape as if caught in the moment, struggling to find the words he longs to express. Witnessing what is happening to his friend, Levi scoots back in awe. As Jones rises from his seat, a shimmering aura envelops him, and he gently ascends three feet above the ground, defying gravity with an effortless grace. The bluish sludge lurking beneath the sandy surface bubbles ominously, releasing a faint, acrid scent as the heat makes it churn and swirl. As if in unison, the spiders on the ceiling scurry away. An echoing moan escapes from Jones as the sludge boils while he rotates in a circle above it. From the murky depths of the blue, boiling sludge, six ethereal figures of miners rise. Their translucent forms shimmer with a faint, otherworldly glow. As they ascend, an eerie light dances around them, casting shadows that flicker like memories in the steam-laden air. They hold tools that faintly shimmer in their hands, their almost transparent surfaces catching the light.

In a haunting tableau, one spectral miner lifts his vaporous pickaxe above his head. With a deliberate swing, he brings it down; the point slicing through the empty air. The remaining ghosts, ethereal figures cloaked in a haunting mist, lift their spectral pickaxes in unison, the cold metal glinting in the dim light. With a slow, synchronized motion, they swing their tools downward. Ching! Ching! Ching! As Levi stands frozen, he watches in horror as the spectacle unfolds. Emerging from nothingness, a shimmering blue track forms as ethereal ghosts skillfully swing their pickaxes, leaving behind a glimmering trail that dances in the air.

The ghostly figures are building a mystical bridge leading to the crystal. They swing their tools even more quickly. Upon completion of the track, a collection of sturdy wood, sleek metal, and gleaming wheels arrives before Levi. Workers neatly stack the raw materials, preparing them for transformation into something extraordinary. Jones continues to spin in the air in a zombie-like state. Soon, the specters move over to Levi and assemble the mine cart. Levi cannot speak. Everything ends as suddenly as it started. The meticulously crafted enchanting cart, illuminated by an otherworldly blue glow, is now complete. The miners disappear back into the bubbling blue sludge in an instant. As Jones slowly descends toward the earth, a flicker of awareness stirs within him.

"What, what happened?"

"You were floating again... there were more ghost miners... and now this track."

Jones looks at the semitransparent ghostly mine cart and tracks.

"We must hop in."

"Something told me you would say that. Come on."

As soon as the boys settle into the creaky mine cart, it jolts to life, lurching forward with a rumble that echoes through the cavern. The blue ooze bubbles once more as the cart rolls down the track. Steam and bubbles violently erupted from the sandy ground, hissing and popping in a chaotic dance. The intense heat distorted the air, while a terrible moaning sound echoed ominously, sending shivers down Levi's spine.

"What's going on?"

"I'm not sure, but I wasn't expecting this."

Eerie, phantasmal hands emerge from the viscous ooze, their translucent fingers twisting and stretching as if yearning for something beyond their grasp. The eerie wails echo through the air, growing louder with each passing moment. From the depths beneath the track, grotesque ghouls emerge, their twisted forms and hollow eyes spreading fear through the air. They resemble the previous miners, but they appear much more frightening. In the haunting scene, faces void of eyes, mouths wide open, release chilling cries that fill the room with dread. Levi screams as the ghostly vehicle nears the shard. A dense, eerie fog suddenly appears, wrapping around the landscape. Jones has a worried expression, but he stays calm. Levi struggles to remain quiet.

"Faster, Faster. How do we go faster?"

Jones seems to fall back into a trance.

"Almost there."

Levi skillfully evades the ghost's outstretched, ethereal hands, feeling the cold air ripple past him as they narrowly miss their mark. Meanwhile, Jones remains utterly fixated on the shimmering shard before him, oblivious to the haunting presence surrounding them. From the swirling depths of the fog, the ancient Miner emerges, his spectral form shimmering in the blue light. He hovers gracefully above the glowing ooze that bubbles ominously beneath him. Gritting his broken teeth, he watches the boys as they approach the glowing fragment. The amulet hanging from the Miner's neck gleams with a vivid, pulsing light, its radiance seeming to beat in rhythm with his tainted heart.

"Yes. Yes. I feel the power. Quickly, touch it! Touch the shard!"

Jones points his index finger forward with his left arm in a straight and firm gesture. The mine cart slowly approaches the shard. After reaching the midpoint of the track, the cart stops. Levi asks what is happening. Jones wears a puzzled expression for a moment before he solves the problem.

"We have to jump to reach the shard. I'm unable to move."
"Jump? What do you mean you're unable to move? "

Jones points to the bottom of the mine cart, where blue fluid is slowly leaking into it. Like a scene pulled from a nightmare, the track and bridge seem to disappear into the murky depths, swallowed whole by the relentless grip of the quicksand beneath them.

"You've got to be kidding me."

A minor anxiety attack strikes Levi as he looks forward.

"OK. OK. I can do this. I can't believe I'm doing this. I can't believe I'm doing this."

He steadies himself on the cart's edge, his heart racing as he prepares to leap. With a deep breath, he launches into the air, his feet finding the jagged shard below. However, the surface is slick and unstable, causing him to lose his balance. For a terrifying moment, he teeters on the brink, nearly plunging into the viscous, swirling fluid that churns ominously beneath him. Unfazed by the danger Levi is in, Jones gives him further instruction.

"Touch the tip of the shard."

Levi calls out to Jones, urging him to extend his hand and make the leap. With a firm grip, he seizes Jones's hand. He pulls him forward, forcing him onto the precarious shard just as the mine cart and its rusty tracks vanish into the thick, sludgy blue ooze below. The murky substance swallows everything in its path, sending ripples across its surface as if to mock their narrow escape.

Chapter 9

Levi and Jones grasp firmly onto the jagged shard, their fingers wrapping around its sharp edges as if it were a lifeline in a turbulent sea. Levi shifts his focus to the shard. His gaze locked onto its jagged surface. With a deliberate movement, he raises his hand high above his head, the soft blue glow glinting off the edges of the shard. His pointer finger extends slowly, almost reverently, until it hovers just above the sharp tip. With a last surge of determination, he lunges forward, barely grazing the tip of the shard with his fingertip. A deep, guttural rumble shakes the air, reverberating through the surroundings like an ominous growl. Startled, they scan the area, their hearts racing as they search for the elusive source of the unsettling sound. A swirling mass of flies, buzzing insects, and aggressive hornets pours into the chamber, invading through a network of concealed openings in the walls.

Their frantic wings create a deafening hum, filling the air with palpable tension as they swarm, casting a dark, chaotic shadow over the once serene space. A brilliant radiance radiates from Jones' amulet, casting an enchanting glow that dances around him. Sand whirls around the massive boulder, swirling in graceful eddies and spirals reminiscent of water cascading down a toilet bowl, lost in its relentless journey. Each grain dances in the air, creating a mesmerizing spectacle as the shard shakes and sinks. As the boys tumble from the shard, they thrash wildly, their arms and legs flailing in a desperate struggle to keep themselves above the suffocating sea of sand that threatens to swallow them whole. Their faces twist in panic as the grains cling to their skin. They search for something solid to grasp, fighting against the overwhelming weight of the shifting sand.

"Help Jones! Help!"

They cry as the swirling sand forcefully propels them down toward a mysterious siphon, concealing their heads from view. While they descend into the depths of the suffocating siphon, they finally land with a soft thud on a stretch of fine, golden sand about twelve feet below the surface. The air is thick and warm, wrapping around them like a heavy blanket. Gasping for fresh air, they find themselves in a hidden chamber unseen for centuries. They pick themselves up and dust each other off, looking around. This strange room is unlike anything they have seen, so they explore it.

In the dim glow of low-light torches flickering softly from enormous earthen pots scattered across the ground, twisted rock formations rise majestically, their shadows dancing along the uneven surfaces. Small pools of shimmering water catch the light, reflecting the surreal surroundings, while colossal roots intertwine like ancient serpents, anchoring themselves in the rugged terrain. Odd, vibrant plants sprout defiantly from crevices, their bio luminescent hues adding an otherworldly charm. The air is thick with an intricate tapestry of dense, silken webbing that clings to the ceiling and walls, creating a delicate, almost ethereal veil that hints at hidden mysteries waiting to be uncovered.

Broken pottery shards, remnants of a bygone culture, lie scattered like forgotten memories, further enriching this enchanting yet eerie subterranean landscape.

The chamber stretches out like a lengthy corridor, its walls rising above. Beneath layers of dirt and scattered bones lies an exquisite mosaic-tiled floor, vibrant with intricate patterns that tell stories of a long-forgotten era. Dozens of skeletons lie scattered across the ground for nearly a hundred feet; any experienced explorer could easily mistake this for a tomb. As if eternally stationed to safeguard this area, the skeletal figures clutch corroded weapons, their once-glorious edges dulled and jagged from ages past. They still grasp decaying shields, their surfaces marred by rot and the ravages of time, embodying a haunting reminder of forgotten battles. These silent sentinels remain in their perpetual slumber, an eerie testament to their ultimate resting place. The boys eagerly stand on a mound of sand and rocks, absorbing the mysterious chamber as ancient torches flicker to life. As Jones oscillates between consciousness and a zombie-like state, Levi takes a deep, enthusiastic breath.

"Where are we now?"

"This is the chamber that we need to be in. It's here."

"What's here?"

Jones points to the opposite end of the chamber.

"The treasure."

Levi and Jones move cautiously down the shadowy hallway. They are careful about where they step to avoid disturbing the bones of the carcasses. Levi cringes as they pass over several dozen skulls glaring at them.

"This is scary, Jones."

As the boys carefully pick their way through the bones, the air is heavy with anticipation, Jones trailing behind Levi, his face a mask of stoic indifference and his eyes devoid of emotion. Time seems to stretch, making the moment feel like hours. As they get closer to the area Jones had indicated, they cast cautious glances around, wary of any hidden traps amidst the rugged gray and bronze rock formations. A perfectly square object catches their eye, its sharp lines starkly contrasting the weathered textures of the surrounding minerals and jagged stones. The rocks, shaped by time and elements, form a dramatic backdrop. Meanwhile, with its geometric precision, the square object stands out as an anomaly, both out of place and intriguing in this natural landscape.

The object cloaked in delicate layers of tattered fabric hangs loosely and appears threadbare in places. Delicate strands of cobwebs weave intricately across its surface, glistening faintly in the light. Jones takes a confident step forward, positioning himself on a rugged elevation of broken stones that jut at odd angles. With painstakingly cautious movements, he carefully nudges aside the tattered fabric and entwined webbing, uncovering a magnificent treasure chest. Intricate copper straps, shimmering in the dim light, adorn the chest; its surface gleams with a rich patina, hinting at the riches within.

Exquisite gemstones, each sparkling with unique brilliance, elegantly embellish the copper straps. Interspersed among these jewels are fiery opals, their colors shifting from vibrant oranges to deep reds, creating a stunning contrast against the warm luster of the copper. In such a desolate place as this, something so beautiful amazes the two. An ornate golden lock, its surface glimmering with intricate diamond embellishments that catch the light beautifully, firmly fastens the lid. However, it presents a puzzling mystery, for there is no keyhole to unlock its secrets. Levi stands before it, his brow furrowed in confusion.

"That's odd. I know we don't have a key, but there is nowhere to put one."

They wonder what to do when Jones' amulet rapidly shifts from a dull glow to a bright flash. Fear takes over Levi.

"What's happening?"

"I'm not sure."

A haunting moan fills the silent chamber as the guys glance around for the source. Levi is the first to sense a gentle breeze sweeping through the room.

"Not again!"

Jones carries a confused look.

"I don't know what's going on."

A vibrant green spot illuminates the surroundings in the center of the chamber on the ground, pulsating rhythmically as it slowly spins. The boys struggle to hold on to the treasure chest as the breeze turns into a strong wind. The air around the chamber quivers with an eerie energy as every skeleton and scattered pile of bones tremble. It vibrates, creating a haunting symphony of rattles and clinks. The flickering shadows dance across the walls, casting an unsettling glow that highlights the grim parade of skeletal remains, each seemingly alive with a restless, otherworldly motion. The green spot suddenly behaves like a vacuum, pulling everything toward it.

As the green spot pulls the bones into itself, it expands into a larger hole, emitting a bright green hue. From the scattered bones drawn into its swirling vortex, a colossal spectral figure takes shape, its ethereal form rising gracefully toward the apex of the miniature tornado, shimmering with an otherworldly glow. The air crackles with energy as it levitates, a haunting silhouette winding upward against the backdrop of the corridor. Towering approximately eight feet tall, this figure vividly captures the full-bodied representation of a Miner, showcasing the rugged details of his attire and the determination in his stance. Blood flows through the miners' veins in sync with the pulses of Jones' amulet. He grits his shattered teeth as saliva oozes from his weathered, chapped lips. The Miner opens his eyes with a menacing glare. Seeing the boys, he grins wickedly and laughs hauntingly. He salivates as he looks at the boys.

"It's almost complete."

Having regained his composure, Levi wants answers.

"What's almost complete?"

The Miner points to the treasure chest while arguing with Levi.

"Open the chest, now!"

"How? There is no keyhole in the lock."

"Take the amulet, Jones, and place it against the lock."

Jones mumbles as he removes the amulet from his neck and inches it closer to the lock.

"Something is not right."

A look of deep concentration etches itself onto the Miner's face, his eyes widening in alarm as he listens intently to Levi and Jones engaged in their conversation.

"What do you mean, something isn't right?"

"Well, look at him, Levi. This isn't the ghost we first met down here."

The Miner becomes angrier and yells at the boys.

"Hurry!"

They are both startled by the sudden outburst. As Jones approaches the lock, the amulet glows brighter, and little green orbs manifest and float around it.

"Faster, Faster!"

Without warning, Levi lunges forward, seizing Jones' wrist just inches from the lock. His voice pierces the tension in the air as he shouts at the Miner, urgency blazing in his eyes.

"Hold on! When we open this lock, how do we know that you won't hurt us and that we can go back home?"

The Miner's eyes turn red as if a fire is lit behind them. He clenches his teeth until some of them crack, and he balls his fist.

"If you don't open the chest, I will finish you here! It's almost complete!"

Levi looks back at Jones.

"I don't trust him either, but it looks like we have no choice."

Levi pulls his hand away, and Jones carefully lifts the amulet and touches the lock. As the ancient amulet brushes against the intricately designed lock, a surge of energy courses through it, releasing a brilliant flash of emerald light that momentarily envelopes the boys. The intense glow fills the air with a haunting radiance, casting eerie shadows around them and leaving them momentarily blinded. Their hearts race wildly, caught in a thrilling dance of fear and awe. The earth trembles beneath them, and a deep rumble resonates in the air, causing dust to swirl around Jones. In an instant, the ethereal glow of the amulet flickers and sputters, its brilliance dimming before it vanishes entirely. Moments later, it reappears, casting a shimmering light as it attaches itself to Jones' neck, settling there as if it had never left. He seems to be out of the trance and acting like himself again. He looks around, surprised and confused.

"What's going on? Where are we?"

With a creaking and rusty grinding noise, the lock finally gives way, tumbling to the ground as it falls away from the chest. The Miner laughs.

"It is done. Finally, after all these years, I have it."

Levi and Jones locked eyes, an unspoken tension hanging in the air as they tried to decipher the cryptic words. What could he possibly mean? The question lingered between them, thickening the atmosphere with curiosity and unease. The chest lid opens halfway, and their eyes widen in surprise. A radiant, glassy orb with a brilliant white hue gracefully emerges from within the chest, ascending slowly into the air. As it floats toward the back of the room, it emits a soft, melodic hum that fills the space with an enchanting resonance. The gentle light from the orb casts delicate reflections on the walls, creating a mesmerizing dance of brightness as it moves. All other sounds fade away as the orb floats through the air. The air turns crisp and cool, a noticeable shift in temperature that sends a shiver down their spines. Then, in a sudden twist, the orb radiates a blinding light, forcing the boys to squint and shield their eyes from its brilliance. With a swift motion, Jones gestures away from Levi, his finger tracing the path of the glowing sphere as it gracefully drifts behind the ancient chest. He barely stammers out a word.

"What is that?"

A radiant white orb shatters into countless shimmering fragments, each glimmering with ethereal light as it gradually reshapes into a man's figure. A unique blend of armor and clothing, crafted from various animal hides, adorns the man, who exudes a non-threatening aura. His attire, unlike anything the Miner has ever seen, tells a story of both strength and harmony with nature. An intricate headdress sits atop his head, a masterpiece of feathers cascading down like vibrant waterfalls, intertwined with majestic antlers and accents of gleaming copper that catch the light. His footwear is striking, resembling the massive paws of a bear, each step he takes echoing a powerful presence while simultaneously evoking a sense of connection to the wild. He is a weathered Tribal Guardian, his features etched with the lines of countless seasons, a sentinel of ancient wisdom. The Miner stares in astonishment, taken aback by the unexpected encounter with this timeless figure.

"What is this, foul magic? What is happening?"

As the brightness of the transformation fades, the Guardian gazes at the boys. Rage consumes the Miner.

"Who are you?"

The Guardian answers.

"Igmar mo tazafran shuly,"

The Miner is tired of playing games with the spirit.

"What is this language you speak?"

Jones looks at Levi.

"I don't understand him, do you?"

Levi shakes his head and turns to the Guardian as the ghostly Miner approaches.

"I don't have time for this!"

The solid spirit mass yells with anger as he glares at the prospector.

"Silence!"

The ethereal figure then addresses Levi and Jones, its voice a haunting whisper that seems to weave through the air, filling the space with a chilling yet mesmerizing presence.

"I will now speak your dialect. I am Yoshdamya (Yo-sha-da-my-a), the revered Guardian entrusted with protecting the sacred contents held within this ancient chest. I have patiently anticipated this moment for countless millennia, each passing year deepening my longing for its arrival. The item locked away within this chest is beyond comprehension, pulsating with an intensity that seems to defy the very laws of nature. Each moment spent in its presence hints at unimaginable potential, calling out to those who dare to seek its secrets."

The Miner lunges forward with an outstretched hand, interrupting the spirit in his attempt to seize the treasure.

"And it's mine!"

A dazzling explosion of radiant light erupts in the room, enveloping everything in a blinding glow. The force of the burst sends the Miner reeling backwards. His body propelled several feet as he staggers, momentarily dazed by the overwhelming brightness. Meanwhile, the Guardian's voice rang out, filled with urgency and power, cutting through the chaos.

"BACK!"

A tremor of fear mixed with the purity of innocence washes over Levi's face as he gazes up at the towering figure of the Guardian. His wide eyes shimmer with desperation, and a quiver enters his voice as he pleads for mercy.

"We have been through so much. We were trying to escape a storm when we met this Miner who forced us here. Finding whatever is in this chest almost killed us. Please tell us what it is so we can go home."

The guardian nods and then speaks.

"Countless millions of years ago, this revered planet was a barren landscape inhabited by only a handful of life forms. The air was still and silent, and the terrain was marked by vast stretches of untouched wilderness, where simple organisms roamed in harmony with the primordial elements of Earth. Amid an expansive and barren stretch of land, a solitary tree soared high into the sky, its gnarled branches reaching out like arms in search of solace. Surrounded by a barren, rugged landscape, it stood as a lone sentinel, resilient against the harsh winds and unyielding elements. This resilient tree thrived against all odds in its unforgiving environment, where the parched soil offered scant water. Its many branches stretched wide, creating a sturdy silhouette against the sky. A soft, ethereal glow emitted a pale white light, illuminating its surroundings and lending an other-worldly quality to its majestic presence. The area around this important tree became a wide space of emptiness, extending fifty fathoms in all directions. No grass, wildflowers, or even tough weeds grew in this empty area, as if the soil had lost its strength because of the tree's powerful presence."

Yoshdamya gazes into the horizon.

"As time passed, a forest grew around the tree, yet its boundaries remained unaffected by other roots. Ancient legend describes the tree's leaves as reaching the heavens, with vibrant green canopies stretching toward the sky as if embracing the clouds above. Neither fog nor cloud could keep the sunlight from shining on it. This revered hardwood structure has withstood earthquakes and natural disasters for centuries. Over thousands of years, as humanity changed, a troubling madness grew in people's minds. This madness came from the mysterious appeal of the sacred tree. Despite their efforts, they could not get close enough to harvest it or cause it harm. In the lush grove surrounding the ancient tree, the creatures that called it home established a sanctuary. Birds flitted from branch to branch, and small mammals scurried through the underbrush, all thriving in this sheltered environment. Although this sacred space protected the animals, it did not offer humans the same protection. Throughout history, people have passed down stories about its legacy and power."

The Miner slowly opens his eyes, their depths revealing determination and grit. He rises to his feet, dust and rubble cascading off his shoulders with each movement. With a swift, commanding gesture, he raises his hand, summoning nearby loose chunks of rock. The stones respond to his silent command, tumbling through the air with a menacing grace, hurtling toward the imposing figure of the Guardian.

"Enough of this storytelling! Give me the treasure!"

Another blinding flash of light erupts, engulfing the area instantly. The air crackles with tension as the Guardian's voice booms.

"BACK!"

The flying rocks rush back toward the Miner, knocking him down and stunning him again. The Guardian continues telling the boys the legend.

"Man referred to this ancient timber as The Tree of Time, a name that evoked its enduring presence and the countless stories it had witnessed over the ages. Once, there was an ancient tribesman who disguised himself by hiding under a bear fur to deceive a tree. He got close enough to the tree to touch it, but when he did, his tribe never saw him again. Beings from beyond this world brought it here. It had existed for millions of years until one day a great fiery ball fell from the sky. The ground opened up and began swallowing the tree. The tree's glow flickered. As the ancient tree succumbed to the earth's embrace, its once-robust trunk weakened, slowly surrendering to the weight of the soil as the ground enveloped its roots. In a moment of urgency, a tribesman raced toward the tree, his heart pounding with the realization that time was running out. With swift, decisive motions, he wielded his trusty axe and severed a small piece of the gnarled root just before it disappeared into the dark depths below. Clutching the precious fragment tightly, he turned and hurried away, disappearing into the underbrush, destined to be lost to both the tree and time forever."

Suddenly, the chest opens all the way up. Inside the elegantly crafted wooden box lies a captivating display of spider webs, their intricate patterns glistening in the light. Beneath this delicate webbing, a luxurious golden cloth shines with warmth and richness, creating a striking contrast. The object they discover inside strikes the boys, their eyes wide with astonishment. What Levi sees leaves him confused about this spectacle.

"What in the world is that?"

Jones disappointingly responds.

"It looks like a stick."

A gnarled, heavy piece of wood, tinged with grime and marked by deep knots, rises gracefully from the chest. Its subtle curve suggests a story of resilience. Two powerful eagle claws grip it, anchoring the rugged wood in place as if it were a precious artifact of nature. The object measures approximately fourteen inches, exuding an earthy aroma reminiscent of the rich soil from which it emerged. Levi shouts over to the Miner, who is stirring from his daze and slowly realizing his surroundings.

"I can't believe this. Is this what we went through all of this nightmare for?"

The Guardian intervenes.

"This is a piece of the root from the Tree of Time."

With determination, the prospector leaps to his feet, his eyes locked onto the coveted root. Fueled by excitement and greed, he charges forward, ready to claim his prize.

"It's mine, and I'm taking it now!"

The Guardian lifted his hands high and shouted again.

"Back!"

In an instant, a blinding flash of light erupts, sending the Miner reeling and leaving him momentarily disoriented. With a gentle and steady ascent over the chest, the root spins delicately, as if performing a mesmerizing dance. With a glimmer of insight in his eyes, the wise entity dives deeper into the conversation, captivating the boys.

"This root is all that remains of the tree, and it holds tremendous power. It is unclear how much power it possesses, but I am certain you will learn more about it as time passes. Whenever it is located, its protectors can travel back in time."

Levi and Jones appear shocked and confused. Jones raises his hand.

"Time travel?"

"Whenever you find yourself on the surface of the Earth, you can reach out to the root, summoning forth the living shadows of history that linger in the very place where you stand. These echoes of the past, rich with emotion and stories untold, intertwine with the present, revealing the intricate tapestry of life that once thrived in that very spot."

Jones expresses that he still doesn't understand until Levi chimes in.

"Oh, I get it. If we are standing somewhere in the city of, say, Detroit, we could use the root to take us back in time before Detroit was ever a city."

"You have the wisdom of a man ten times your age. The root grants you the power to alter time's shadow, and if you are around it long enough, your body may absorb some of its power. You cannot stop time. Now, young Guardians, what I will share with you is very important, so please listen carefully. Whenever there is stress in the flow of time, the root will summon you to wield its power to promote good and just deeds. This power brings along significant responsibilities that can be both demanding and complex. It requires careful consideration and the willingness to navigate difficult situations, as the choices made can have far-reaching consequences."

Levi and Jones look at one another, their jaws drop.

"Guardians?"

"It is your destiny to protect the root and all time. As the new Guardians of the root, it will attach to you, and only you will be able to use its power."

Jones murmurs in confusion.

"But hold on, if it has powers that its protector can use, why are you stuck guarding it in a chest?"

"I took a vow to protect the root until you two found it."

Their jaws drop even further as Jones stares at the root.

"What? Us two?"

"Yes, you two. A prophecy foretold, many millennia ago, that two young future Guardians, Levi and Jones, would find and protect the root; everything happens for a reason."

The boys are in awe of hearing this news. The Miner finally regains consciousness, fury blazing in his eyes more intense than ever before. With determination burning in his eyes, he rises to his feet, channeling every ounce of his energy into his next bold move. He tries to push the boys out of the way using his powers.

"Don't touch it, move!"

With a fluid motion, he raises his hand, and massive boulders lift off the ground, their surfaces glimmering in the light. The air crackles with energy as the boulders hurl forward, hurtling like meteors aimed at the tribal Guardian. Just before they collide, the Guardian seems to evaporate into thin air, leaving nothing but a faint shimmer in the space where he once stood. With a swift motion, he reaches down and clutches the thick, gnarled root protruding from its position above the chest. Levi and Jones quickly dart to the side of the earthen mound that conceals the weathered chest beneath layers of soil and rock. With a hearty laugh, he glares fiercely at Levi, Jones, and the Guardian, who has just reappeared.

"This simple stick grants me limitless power! It can manipulate time, allowing me to return and make myself incredibly rich and powerful. Finally, I can escape this mine for good!"

Still hiding behind the treasure chest, Jones yells at the prospector.

"What do you mean?"

In his malevolent gaze, the Miner regards Jones.

"Oh, I'm sorry. Didn't I introduce myself? I'm really Orville Crenshaw, a self-proclaimed philanthropist, renowned archaeologist, and soon-to-be the most powerful being on earth. I discovered the rumored legend about this root over one hundred years ago. You, the so-called Guardians, have just aided me in uncovering the legendary treasure once deemed a myth—the most powerful artifact of all time!"

Levi becomes extremely angry.

"You lied to us!"

Crenshaw laughs at Levi's attempt to be courageous.

"Those idiot miners couldn't do the job, and I was stuck here, but you two gullible little children put it right in my hands. Now it's time for you to die!"

He waves the root at the boys, and the Guardian raises his staff.

"Back!"

A sudden bright light knocks Crenshaw off his feet. As he tumbles backward, the root slips from his grasp, hitting the ground with a thud. In a flurry of excitement, the boys dive to snatch it up just as Crenshaw rises to his feet, launching into an animated chant of dialogue that fills the air with energy. His eyes turn red and glow. The ground trembles and the hole from which he emerged widens. They listen to the wailing spirits as the hole expands. The earth trembles with such ferocity that the boy's struggle to stand, their bodies thrown about helplessly. Fear grips their hearts as they exchange wide-eyed glances, each one unable to suppress the rising tide of panic that courses through them. The world around them feels like it's erupting, and they cling desperately to the ground, hoping for elusive stability. Levi shouts at Crenshaw.

"No! You said we could leave when we found it!"

From the depths of the dark hole, the eerie remains of ancient guards rise, their skeletal figures illuminated by the flickering light. As the chilling scene unfolds, Crenshaw looms ominously over the boys, his voice a low growl filled with menace.

"You can't escape, and I'll keep you trapped here forever!"

Before the boys stood a chilling sight—fifty skeletons clad in tattered ancient robes and fragments of rusted armor. Their hollow eye sockets seem to smolder with a ghostly light as if beckoning the brave or foolish to venture closer. Harnessing his extraordinary power, Crenshaw effortlessly lifts the root into the air, watching as it floats before him before returning to his outstretched hands. He then orders the skeletons to attack.

"Enough games! It's time for you to die!"

With a fierce battle cry, they surge toward the boys, swords raised high and shields locked together in perfect formation. Levi and Jones cling to each other, their hearts racing as fear washes over them. The Guardian brandishes his staff, and just as the nearest skeleton advances toward the boys, a brilliant flash and deafening crackle fill the air. However, despite the display of magic, the skeletons remain unfazed and continue their relentless pursuit of the boys. The Guardian has a shocked and distressed expression on his face. Crenshaw laughs.

"You can't stop me! I will be all-powerful and control time."

He extends his arm gracefully, palm facing upward, and the root gently rises, suspended in mid-air just above his hand. It rotates slowly in a clockwise motion, each turn accompanied by a rhythmic pulsation of vibrant energy that seems to shimmer with a haunting glow. The Guardian looks at the boys and apologizes.

"I'm sorry. I can't protect you from the powers of the root."

He raised his staff high, channeling all his strength to repel the swirling magic unleashed by Crenshaw. But despite his desperate efforts, the dark power overwhelmed him, leaving him vulnerable and defeated. Laughing diabolically, Crenshaw grabs the spinning root and points it at poor Levi and Jones.

"I am all powerful! You have done my bidding and now you will suffer an untimely death! There is nothing you can do. Die!"

A vibrant beam of lethal magic surges from the root, racing toward Jones with menacing speed. Heart pounding in his chest, Jones instinctively leaps back, seeking refuge behind a towering boulder alongside Levi. They huddle behind cover, their hearts racing as the room trembles violently around them. Crenshaw holds his hand out again as the root spins above it. Another wave of magic shoots toward the boys, causing the boulder behind which they hide to crumble. The tribal Guardian gathers all of his strength and shouts at the prospector.

"Back!"

A more powerful flash of light knocks Orville back several feet, causing him to drop the root. Extending his hand, he uses his magic to pull the root towards him once again. Running back and forth, the boys attempt to avoid the dangerous roots' power; each step is a dance with death. The tension escalates as Crenshaw relentlessly pursues his targets, each encounter more intense than the last, as he attempts to take them down individually. The ground continues to shake as more rocks and boulders break from the chamber, nearly landing on the exhausted youth. Levi pulls Jones out of harm's way.

"Run!"

By that moment, Crenshaw had regained his footing, the enchanted root swirling gracefully above his palm like a vibrant energy vortex. He unleashed another surge of powerful magic with a determined focus, sending it crackling through the air toward the boys, who stood wide-eyed in anticipation of the oncoming spell. As Jones stumbles and topples backward, the surge of magic energy collides with the amulet dangling from his neck. The amulet glows with an intense light, pulsating like a heartbeat, before channeling that energy back toward Orville. The moment is electric, and Orville's eyes widen in horror as he lets out a piercing scream, the sound echoing in the charged chamber.

"No!"

As the magical energy strikes him, Crenshaw's body erupts in a dazzling fireworks display, transforming into a celestial spectacle of millions of sparkling stars. The root falls back to the ground. Both Crenshaw and the amulet around Jones's neck vanished in an instant. The ground continues to convulse. The Guardian lifts his staff aloft, and in an instant, a brilliant cascade of white sparks erupts from its tip, trailing like shooting stars toward the root below. As the glimmering light flickers and swirls, it grabs the root and places it softly in Jones's hand. He lowers his staff and speaks again.

"My time here is done, and now I can rest. The root is yours to protect. Use it wisely. Use it for good. Never let it fall into evil hands."

With that, he then fades away. As the ground shakes harder, rocks break free from the walls of the chamber. Jones grabs Levi's hand and pulls him out of harm's way as they struggle not to be crushed by the falling rock. Clutching onto Jones, Levi screams.

"How do we get out of here?"

The chamber tremors with a ferocity unmatched. The walls tremble violently, dust and debris rain from above, and the air vibrates with a deep, resonant roar, making it feel as if the ground beneath is alive with chaos. As the walls give way, groundwater streams through the jagged cracks, transforming the floor into a dark, swirling pool. Masses of stone tumble down around the boys, crashing just a few feet away, sending dust and debris swirling like a chaotic dance. The water quickly rises and is already up to their waist. Jones shouts fiercely, straining to keep the gnarled root elevated above the water, his muscles tense with effort as he battles against its stubborn weight.

"Hold on to me!"

They feel trapped in a dark fish tank, with water now up to their shoulders. The boys find themselves submerged, fighting against the weight of the water as panic grips them. With every passing moment, their lungs scream for air, and the desperate struggle to break free from the depths becomes a race against time. Hysteria grips them as the reality of their situation sinks in; the chilling, suffocating water surrounds them, and they realize they are moments away from succumbing to the depths. In an electrifying moment, the root bursts into a brilliant white light, swirling above Jones' fingers, which are nearly submerged beneath the surface of the water. A massive boulder, teetering precariously above the boys, suddenly breaks loose, poised to crush them beneath the water's surface. Just as the impending doom seems inevitable, an overwhelming flash of radiant, sparkling light erupts from the swirling root. The brilliance illuminates everything for a fleeting moment before plunging the world into an eerie darkness, enveloping them in silence.

Everything is nothing. Everything is black, and everything is silent. The world fades into an ethereal void where silence envelops everything, and time stands still. Upon opening his eyes, Levi finds himself back in his classroom before the dismissal. The constant noise of a busy classroom persists as if nothing ever altered its course. Levi scans the classroom, noticing his fellow students, and then his gaze settles on Jones, who is looking back at him. They stare at each other in mutual amazement, a connection forming between them as background noise muffles reality. Levi reads Jones's lips.

"What just happened?"

Levi looks around and shrugs his shoulders.

"I don't know!"

The school bell rings earlier than usual as it is a half day that starts the three-day weekend. Mrs. Barren, one of the few English teachers, closes her textbook, lying on top of her desk.

"OK, everyone, class is dismissed. Enjoy your weekend and study for next week's test."

Every student in the room is excited and cheers while gathering their books and bags. They all start walking out to the school buses. They listen to current music playing from various Bluetooth speakers and headphones. The hallway is crowded with kids closing their lockers, and they can hear unwavering excitement, as most are eager to leave early that Thursday morning. Levi and Jones walk out of the classroom, heading into the busy hallway. Feeling in a daze, Levi ponders.

"Are we dreaming?"

"I don't have a clue. I don't think so."

While the students are scrambling around the schoolyard looking for their bus or ride home, some staff members and chaperons are looking out towards the ocean past the school buses, viewing the horizon. It is a beautiful day as the sun reflects off the gentle ocean waves. It is awe-inspiring and brings peace and tranquility to the minds of all who ponder. While walking to their school bus, Jones continues the conversation.

"This is some wicked Déjà vu."

Levi looks around.

"But there is no storm brewing. What happened to it? This isn't what happened before."

"It must have been the root, and we must have flashed back before anything ever happened."

"But it happened, Jones. The caves, the water, the monsters, that Miner! It was all real, wasn't it?"

In a state of confusion, the boys stammered while getting on the bus.

"We aren't crazy, Levi. It was all very real. It seems like a dream, but it has to be real. We must be in a different reality where the storm never happened."

The bus soon departs and, within a few miles, begins dropping off students at their regular stops.

"Well, if it was a dream, that was one heck of a scary adventure."

The bus hits a pothole, and the root sticks out of Levi's bag. He instantly wears a shocked look on his face.

"What the?"

Jones looks around, ensuring that they aren't drawing attention.

"Shhh, see? It wasn't a dream. There's the root."

Before any of the remaining students on the bus notice, Levi stuffs it back into his bag. Soon after, the bus stops in front of Levi's house. Following the bus's departure, Levi stands there for a moment. As he surveys the neighboring homes, he observes a vibrant scene unfolding before him. Residents are bustling about, each engaged in their daily routines. Some are strolling leisurely along the sidewalks, exchanging friendly greetings with one another, while others are tending to their gardens, the vibrant blooms swaying gently in the breeze. The warm sun casts a golden hue over the neighborhood, adding to the cheerful ambiance of this lively community. The rhythmic flow of the ocean waves creates a soothing melody, while seagulls glide effortlessly through the sky, their wings outstretched as if reveling in the air's freedom. The sun glimmers off the water, adding a sparkle to the serene scene, where both land and sea seem to harmonize in perfect tranquility. After inviting Jones into his house, Levi opens his bag to show him the root on the kitchen counter. At that moment, his mom opens the front door.

"Hi, honey. I'm home early. Hey Jones, how are you doing?"

Jones answers as he covers the open backpack, hiding the root.

"Oh, I'm great, Mrs. Lumboss. How are you today?"

"I'm great. I have such exciting news, Levi. I've worked so hard, and it finally paid off. I just accepted a promotion to be a full-time travel blogger for the travel company I work for, and I get to venture all around the world and write about the destinations we sell in the office. You know, Levi, it's almost summer vacation. Your father and I need a break. How would you like to go on a vacation to a different country for the summer? Wouldn't that be exciting? Jones, I'm sure your mother would let you join us. Imagine the fun and adventures that we can have experiencing other cultures and cuisines."

Levis' mother walks into the adjoining room. Jones opens the bag again so that only he and Levi can see the root. They exchange huge grins and high-fives.

Levi answers, "That sounds great, Mom. We can't wait."